IT'S ALL
in the EYES

ENDORSEMENTS

"An enchanting tale of faith, hope, and love. This story illustrates the importance of persevering through tough times and highlights the promise of brighter days ahead. The reader is drawn into the wonderful and varied settings of Crete, Frankfurt, and Ireland. Indeed, this book doubles as something of a travelogue—describing some wonderful places and recommending some tasty-sounding local delicacies. I'm sure this book will encourage readers to undertake some new adventures of their own."

—Pastor Ian Gall
Riverside Evangelical Church, Ayr, Scotland

"A love story set against a backdrop of tragedy and disappointment, *It's All in the Eyes* takes us on a breathtaking journey of hope and joy. From a starter of Crete, followed by a main course of Frankfurt, and finishing with a dessert of Ireland, we are led through a tender, developing relationship that is delightful, innocent, and refreshing. Readers of this book will discover that faith and joy go hand in hand and may well find hope rekindled in their own lives."

—Reverend Bill Ferguson

IT'S ALL
in the EYES

A NOVEL

ROBERT MARK
WALKER

AMBASSADOR INTERNATIONAL
GREENVILLE, SOUTH CAROLINA & BELFAST, NORTHERN IRELAND

www.ambassador-international.com

IT'S ALL IN THE EYES

ISBN: 978-1-64960-510-8
eISBN: 978-1-64960-553-5

Cover Design by Hannah Linder Designs
Interior Typesetting by Dentelle Design
Edited by Bruce Stouffer

Scripture quotations taken from the Holy Bible, New International Version®, NIV®
Copyright ©1973, 1978, 1984, 2011 by Biblica, Inc.® Used by permission. All rights
reserved worldwide.

This is a work of fiction. Names, characters, and incidents are all products of the
author's imagination or are used for fictional purposes. Any resemblance to actual
events or persons, living or dead, is entirely coincidental. Any mentioned brand names,
places, and trademarks remain the property of their respective owners, bear no
association with the author or the publisher, and are used for fictional purposes only.

AMBASSADOR INTERNATIONAL
Emerald House
411 University Ridge, Suite B14
Greenville, SC 29601
United States
www.ambassador-international.com

AMBASSADOR BOOKS
The Mount
2 Woodstock Link
Belfast, BT6 8DD
Northern Ireland, United Kingdom
www.ambassadormedia.co.uk

The colophon is a trademark of Ambassador, a Christian publishing company.

*To the Lord of lords and King of kings, my Savior,
my Redeemer, my all.*

*To my family, especially my darling wife Violeta and son Greg,
whose love and support mean the world to me.*

ACKNOWLEDGMENTS

I must mention the incredible people at Ambassador International. Special thanks especially to my editors, Bruce Stouffer and Katie Smith, who have done an outstanding job. Bruce's expertise, professionalism, and advice, in particular, have been first rate throughout. Thanks also to Anna Riebe Raats and the team for the stunning front cover. I am also indebted to my sister, Zelda Joynes, and my good friend Chris Groves. Their proofreading skills and literary advice have been exceptional.

Much obliged to Brian Muir (Air Image) for the excellent photo on the back cover!

I must also mention my endorsers, Ian Gall and Bill Ferguson. Grateful thanks, guys, for making time in your extremely busy schedules to help in this way. Ian actually did his review on vacation, while Bill had a sermon to prepare in the same week!

I am with you . . . I am your God.

I will strengthen you and help you;

I will uphold you with my righteous right hand.

Isaiah 41:10

PROLOGUE

They call it the death zone. It's the place where human cells actually start to die and the body quite literally breaks down. It's a race against time, for any more than sixteen to twenty hours in here can lead to impaired judgment, heart attacks, strokes, severe altitude sickness, loss of consciousness, and, ultimately, death.

Just over twenty-six thousand feet (eight thousand meters) above sea level is the magic number. Nothing magical about it—it is a scientific fact. The lack of oxygen at this altitude means that human life is unsustainable, the cells dying one by one as each minute passes. Over two hundred dead bodies abandoned on Mount Everest, nearly all to be found in this area, are testimony to this. Yet if you want to ascend the highest mountain in the world, there is no other option.

The majority nowadays do make it, of course, battling on through the pain and fear barriers. It's a struggle for survival, for life, for existence, even for breath, as here there is a different type of starvation. Every step is agony, every breath a wrestle, a struggle to the bitter end. Some will have to turn back, so close to their ultimate goal. Others somehow manage to keep going, bit by bit, persisting and enduring, one step forward, pause, then another. And another, and another, plodding on until finally, they not only feel on top of the world—they *are* on top of the world! The ascent is over; the summit has been reached; and they are now able to look down on the whole of humanity.

For a few brief moments, the exhaustion; the mental, physical, and even spiritual fatigue and depletion; the severe thirst caused by dehydration; and all the other aches and pains are forgotten. They are replaced with pure ecstatic joy, with an incredible sense of achievement and accomplishment. They have made it. They have conquered. Through the pain barrier. Through the death zone. Now, only the hazardous descent remains.

PART ONE

CHAPTER 1
ARRIVAL IN CRETE

It was my best friend, Dave Bloomer, who dropped me off at the international airport, thirteen miles away from Belfast, Northern Ireland's capital, in good time for the afternoon flight to Crete.

"Sorry I had to pull out at the last minute, man," he said as the car came to a halt. "Jacqui's down with the flu, and now the youngest's got it as well."

"No worries, Dave," I replied. "Families come first, always."

"Yeah, but I feel awful about tomorrow, Rob, that I'll not be there with you. That date's always on our minds. You know we'll be thinking and praying for you."

"I'll be fine, Dave. And hey, we'll do it next year without fail, okay? Thanks so much for the lift."

We'd been through thick and thin together over the years, in the ups and downs of life. It was thanks to him and his good wife, Jacqui, that I was here today in one piece. Almost.

I checked in, only to find the flight was delayed for two hours due to the connecting flight being held up in Barcelona. Belfast–Barcelona, Barcelona–Belfast, Belfast–Heraklion, Heraklion–Belfast—they sure put their planes to good use!

It was a four-hour-and-forty-minute flight to Crete, which is ideal, really—not too long and, if you're in the right frame of mind, actually quite enjoyable. I always book the aisle seat on planes as it is handy to go to the restroom, have a stretch, or remove something from the overhead luggage compartment if required. Needless to say, the seat in the middle, which should have been Dave's, was empty; but the window one was occupied, and it was nice to have a little bit of banter for a while. However, I was soon doing what I like to do best on a plane—enjoying a nice cup of tea and snacks and reading the in-flight magazine. There are always excellent feature articles with suggestions for possible future getaways, which never fail to stir my interest.

The flight landed in Crete shortly after 10:10 p.m., and all the exhausted passengers trudged off and headed for their respective hotels. Mine was the luxurious five-star Cretan Cali Beach Resort, which thankfully lived up to its name—a drink on arrival (left for tomorrow) with two chicken and bacon wraps smothered in Caesar dressing in the fridge (devoured on the spot). Ten days in the Mediterranean—what could be better?

So here I was, a thirty-five-year-old man, having booked an action-packed vacation online for the two of us, only to find myself now all on my own. Well, not totally on my own—the activities would provide company of a sort each day through meeting new groups of similarly minded explorers. After unpacking, and showering, and eating, it was time for bed. Then the first of those adventures would begin in the morning.

CHAPTER 2
PREVELI BEACH, PALM FOREST, AND RETHYMNO TOWN

I slept well and was down for breakfast in good time, thus managing to find a seat free on the veranda. The views were stunning, as the hotel is located very close to the beach. Inside, the restaurant was laden with all types of goodies, and I filled a bowl with Greek yogurt and fruit before venturing on to the delicious meats and cheeses, not to mention the toast and honey. It was a five-star hotel; so needless to say, the honey had to be picked from a natural, raw honeycomb made up of those delicious wax cells. I ate the honeycomb, wax and all. Let the vacation begin!

Pick-up was right on time at 8:50 a.m.; and due to the mountainous roads, we initially traveled in a ten-seat minibus before transferring to the main sixty-seat bus for the one-and-a-half-hour journey to Damnioni Beach. From there, it was a thirty-minute boat ride to our first major stop, Preveli Tropical Beach and Palm Forest. The boats were ideally suited for this type of transportation, the hulls literally opening up at the front and dropping down close to the beach, allowing passengers to embark and disembark.

Speaking of honey and honeycombs, we had been advised to grab a spot in the shade shortly after arriving, as the place would become a beehive of activity as the day wore on. After my initial walk exploring the sandy beach and beautiful green river surrounded by palm forests, I headed to the much sought-after front line of perfect shade trees, located close to the beach. There was one space left, about twenty-two yards away.

"Yes, perfect," I said to myself and set off to grab it.

Suddenly, about five meters from it, a beautiful, blonde German girl (judging by her book, which was in German) stepped out from the other side, spread her towel, and took my spot. How annoying! Ah well, I would have to go a little further into the woods to the second line of solar defense, further away from the beach. To be honest, though, all I wanted to do was lie down and read, listen to some music, chill out, and take things easy after the hectic workload back home.

It was a deeply relaxing morning before the return boat journey; and then it was on to the only decent restaurant in the place, which, of course, was totally packed.

"I think we have one seat left, sir. Please, follow me," said the waiter.

He was not wrong; everybody from the tour was there, plus many other locals and tourists. And there was indeed only one little table left, with a rather grumpy-looking person sitting on her own: the blonde German from the beach!

"Sorry," I muttered, "it's the only space left."

Her stare could have killed me stone dead. She didn't say a single word, just looked at me with a face like a Lurgan spade. That didn't worry me. What did concern me was the look in those eyes. This was more than getting a little annoyed at someone invading your space. I could tell from my experience over the past two years of looking at my own face in the mirror that she was hurting really, really deeply. There was a profound sadness in those eyes, an immense pain. She was close to breaking.

Dave and Jacqui, along with my faith and the support of the family, had pulled me from that same place—from my pit of despair. That was the key to the healing, I believed—to listening, to opening up, to trusting and confiding in God and in others, to accepting that life can go on in spite of everything, to moving on or, at least, to trying to move on. I now knew I had a new objective: not, to be sure, to undertake to restore her from the pain she was going through but to get a proper smile out of her, a change of mood, a lightening of the spirit, a touch of joy. Surely, that would be doable. Hence, the following questions ensued:

"Great weather we're having! Did you enjoy the beach? Have you tried the baklava yet? Sure is a busy place, don't you think?"

Of course, none of these worked; no reply was forthcoming whatsoever. She didn't utter a single response or even look at me. It was time for a different approach.

"Dave," I said to her, "my best friend—best man as well, actually—was meant to be here, especially for today. This time last year, we were in Machu Picchu, Peru, doing the four-day Inca Trail. The scenery was astounding: lush, green cloud forest, panoramic views of the neighboring valleys, steep mountain passes, and various Inca ruins to marvel at and explore. We had Quechua porters who would prepare breakfast, pack up camp, catch us up, then literally run past to go on ahead and have lunch ready further along the trail! After an early start on the fourth day, we arrived before sunrise at the Sun Gate and got our first sighting of the magnificent Lost City of the Incas. Then the guide came to the fore, explaining in detail some of the incredible history and culture of the place. He showed us the central plaza flanked by the palace, the Sun Temple, and other important buildings. The views were sensational, the city built on a narrow plateau sandwiched between two mountains, with near-vertical drops on either side. You know, the sad thing is most tourists spend only a day at Machu Picchu, arriving by train in the morning, visiting the site, having lunch, and then returning to Cusco in the late afternoon. Instead, we took our time, soaking up the ambience and feeling of peace the city radiates before descending by bus to Aguas Calientes and booking into a hostel. The town is renowned for its open-air thermal baths, whose curative waters soothed our aching muscles! It was truly blissful to lie back in the steaming water, gazing up at the stars above, then to have a delicious meal and a fabulous night's sleep!

"Anyway, this was Dave's way of helping me through a horrendous anniversary. My wife died of cancer exactly two years ago on this day. It had been diagnosed two months earlier, totally out of the blue; and just like that, in such a short time, she was gone. Five years of bliss, passion, true completeness, true fullness, true love suddenly ended. They told me later she had been pregnant with our first baby; the desire of our hearts was never fulfilled. What a double blow, both gone in the blink of an eye, my dreams shattered like a glass bauble falling off the Christmas tree, disintegrating into hundreds of pieces.

"I'm sorry. I'm getting emotional, tearing up. I really don't know why I'm telling you all this. I haven't really talked with a woman since then. I've never *been* with a woman since then, apart from Dave's wife. And I most certainly have never opened up like this. I don't even know your name, but I sense a real genuineness about you. You've got a lovely heart, a very, very peaceful, kind, gentle nature that has attracted me to you. I'm sorry. I shouldn't say it. No, I am just going to say it, anyway. You're a beautiful person inside. Just like Julie was.

"But you know what got me through it all? Friends, family, and faith—caring friends and a loving family who listened to me, who encouraged me, who made me smile again. I learned to trust even more in God again, and that's not a natural response for those who have been deeply hurt. I grasped the need to have a cheerful heart, which is good medicine, according to the book of Proverbs, as opposed to a crushed spirit, which dries up the bones. I don't know you. But I know you're like me: you're hurting. You're suffering inside. You're miserable and sad. I could just walk away and leave you to it; to wallow in your suffering, in your misery, in your pain. But I'm not like that, and you certainly don't deserve it.

"I sense that you're the victim, the innocent party. I've been through torment—through Everest's death zone, in a sense—my body broken, my life a total battle, a struggle to survive. But listen, I got through it. And you can, too. I made it out of that dark tunnel into the light of a new day, a new hope, a new future, a new life. And you can, too. You certainly deserve to."

A stillness fell over us. I had finished my spiel; and for whatever reason I couldn't work out, I had poured out my heart to a total stranger, babbling away endlessly. How embarrassing. I decided to count quietly to thirty and then leave. She still ignored me, never even looking at me. Twenty-five and counting, five to go . . .

"Ernst dumped me two weeks ago." I nearly didn't hear it; but she had responded, ever so quietly. "He said I was too pushy, always talking about having a family, settling down, making a new life together. We had been going out for almost two years. I loved him. He said he loved me, too. I soon came to realize how easy it is to say those words but not mean them at all, how shallow and hollow he really was. The very next day, after telling me how much he loved me, he was sleeping with another woman. Totally out of the blue—totally unexpectedly—he said he couldn't handle all the hassle—that he'd found someone else who didn't talk about having kids. It was time to move on. Just like that, as if it was no big deal. Dump. End. Move on. He moves on, and I'm left trying to pick up the pieces. I'm left shattered, a total wreck."

She had a slight accent; but really, her English was excellent, almost perfect. She never looked at me once, but I certainly looked at her: the beautiful long, blonde hair; the smooth, pure, golden skin. She was beautifully formed, as every woman is. What a fool her ex was.

"Mom decided I needed to get away somewhere to get over it. I'm a school teacher in training, and there's not much money in that; hence, the late booking to a two-star hotel in Hersonissos. Two stars is a joke. It really doesn't deserve even one. The room is tiny. And the food? Uneatable, just what I needed after all I've been through. I'm fed up."

Just then, I noticed a waiter passing and got his attention. "One baklava with ice cream to share, two raki, and two Greek coffees, please."

Nothing more was said until the dessert and drinks arrived. I carefully separated the baklava in two and pushed it over to her, along with the drinks. It was time to speak.

"Greek baklava is the best in the world," I said. "It'll give you a lift, as will the raki and the coffee. Look, I'm going to stick my neck out here, and you don't have a say. I'm sorry, sometimes this is just what has to be done. Here's the plan. The next part of the tour is Rethymno, which I happen to know is a very picturesque old town, good for shopping, with great coffee shops. We're going to walk around together, pick up something nice for your mom and my family and friends, and have a really strong cup or two of coffee. I'm a property investor and work really hard all year, so I tend to compensate for that by booking fabulous vacations. Dave and I always stay in the top hotels and are usually activity-focused: golf, tennis, tours, water-skiing, whatever. We chose the Cretan Cali Hotel—not far from you, actually—quite close to Hersonissos. It's a beautiful five-star beach resort with superb swimming pools, lush gardens, and spectacular views of the Aegean Sea. The buffet is excellent.

"Tonight, you're dining with me; and afterward, you'll get a taxi home. We'll talk about healing, about moving on, about rebuilding your life, about hope. Please. It would kill two birds with one stone. Oh no, I didn't just say that. You're probably vegan. What I meant to say is that I cannot be on my own tonight. It's the second anniversary since . . . it's all too raw. You would . . . really be helping me, and, hopefully, it would be the same for you. I'm sorry, I haven't been like this for ages. I haven't been like this . . . ever."

It was time for that thirty-second countdown again. I had to let her think it through and make her own decision. The thirty seconds passed in total silence. It would have to be thirty more.

"I'm not vegan," she finally replied.

"Yeah, sorry about that. My name's Rob, by the way."

She was getting better. This time, the pause lasted only twenty seconds.

"I'm Gabby. I'd like to join you in Rethymno and for dinner tonight. Thank you."

Progress! No smile, but still progress, her voice a lot stronger than it was ten minutes ago.

En route to our next destination, the bus stopped briefly at the Kourtaliotiko Gorge for a look at the wild, natural landscape. I'd noticed on disembarking that there was an empty space beside her; as we stood together admiring the view, I ventured a question.

"I see there's a free seat beside you on the bus," I said. "Mind if I join you?"

"Be my guest," came the reply, along with a half-smile.

It was on to Rethymno. We found some delightful souvenir shops and picked out a nice present for our moms and Jacqui: night and face cream made from fern extract and the local olive and argan oils the island is famous for. We threw in a few packets of baklava and T-shirts for Dave and Gabby's brother, and that was that. We stopped in the aptly named Brew Your Mind Full coffee shop for some more delicious coffee and a good chat. She told me a little about herself and her family: about how her mom was fluent in Spanish, having worked in the German embassy in Madrid; about her twin brother, Stefan, who was crazy about soccer.

But I did most of the talking, ranting on about previous vacations with Dave, which inevitably led to my next big question: "Doing anything tomorrow?"

"Not really," she replied.

"Have you been to Agios Nikolaos yet?" I asked.

"Not yet."

"You know, today's trip is rated among the top twelve must-dos in Crete. Agios Nikolaos is in the top six. It's a definite must; the lake and town are stunning. The thing is, Gabby, for some reason, I didn't cancel Dave's tickets for the different tours. I'd rather not do them on my own, and I'd rather not let tomorrow's extra ticket go to waste. What do you think? Would you like to join me? As I said, it is highly rated; and you'd be doing me a big favor."

The inevitable pause followed. "I'll think about it," finally came the reply.

Could have been worse, I suppose. Patience, man, patience—a virtue seldom found in women and never in men. Or is it the other way around?

Anyway, she'd agreed to dinner, and that turned out well. I could see right away how impressed she was with the hotel—the massive marble lobby with the luxury sofas, the well-kept gardens bursting with color and incredible aromas, the beautiful pool laden with sun loungers and umbrellas. There was even a water aerobics class in full swing, the Latino music blaring out at full beat. The room impressed her as well—very spacious and clean, with twin beds, an *en suite* bathroom, and superb views of the sea through one window and of the gardens through another.

"Look, there are plenty of towels to share; just go in, lock the door, and take a shower or whatever," I said. "I'll go after you. Get all that sand out."

But it was the five-star buffet that impressed her the most, with the tables laden with every type of food imaginable. I could almost see her mouth watering as we walked around the different sections:

the appetizers, followed by the main courses, and finally the desserts. We managed to get a table out on the veranda, with views of the beach, sea, and a small landmass in the distance called Dia Island.

The meal was a great success, and the conversation began to flow after an initial shaky start. It was fun getting to know each other better and exploring our backgrounds, interests, and likes and dislikes. Maybe it was for the best, but we didn't actually get around to talking about healing or anything else I had planned.

As the evening drew to a close, she finally uttered the words I had been longing to hear: "I think I would enjoy the trip tomorrow. Would that be okay?"

"Oh, Gabby, that's fantastic. I'll come with you in the taxi just to be sure of where to pick you up tomorrow. Should be a great day. Bring your swimsuit, by the way."

It was a short ride from the hotel to Hersonissos. She gave me a lovely half-smile and wave as we departed. On the journey back, sitting in the back seat of the taxi, I pondered everything that had happened in the last few hours. It should have been a really difficult day for me, full of pain, sorrow, and sadness. And yet it was almost the opposite. I wondered what Julie would make of it, looking down from above. And I suddenly realized that she would be happy for me, knowing that it was indeed time to move on into the light of a new era. She would want that. Then the tears began to flow. But they were no longer tears of despair and depression. They seemed more like tears of joy.

"I still miss you, babe. I miss you so, so much."

CHAPTER 3
AGIOS NIKOLAOS

What a day! Right away, after picking up Gabby and other tourists in Hersonissos, the fun began. We sat three rows back and were immediately confronted by two big guys in the row in front.

"I'm Jinky, spelled with a *J*," said the first one in his deep Middlesbrough accent.

"I'm Didge," said the other. "We had a rough one last night, too much beer and curry. Could be a little loud on the bus, if you know what I mean!"

"Got your clothespins ready?" added Jinky as the two of them rolled over, killing themselves laughing.

"Woof, you can still smell the beer fumes. Should be an interesting trip," I whispered into Gabby's ear. I wasn't wrong.

The tour guide sat in the front seat, a big woman who introduced herself as Bertha, from Stuttgart, Germany. She said she would be speaking in both German and English and was on her first spiel when Jinky turned around to us.

"Watch this," he said. Bertha was engrossed in her story and didn't notice a thick hand appear through the seat and attach itself to her shoulder, giving it a shake. She didn't bat an eye—or a vocal cord, for that matter—as she grasped the hand and pushed it firmly away. But Jinky was not to be beaten. She was in full flow again when two enormous hands appeared from either side of the seat, fixing themselves tightly onto each shoulder. The shaking was now even more intense.

"We are now . . . *passing*"—here there was a definite increase in volume—"the . . . the . . . part of the coast known as . . ."

We never found out what that part of the coast was called. She managed to rip off the hands, stand up, and confront Jinky head on. "You do that again, pal, and I'll report you to the police! Get to the back of the bus, both of you!" And off they went, tails between their legs, properly put in their places.

Agios Nikolaos, noted for its famous lake at the center of the town, was a delight to visit. We walked all around the placid water, climbing steeply at one point and then seeing fabulous views of the lake, bridge, town, and Mirabello Bay. The islands in the distance twinkled from the sun's rays reflecting off the ocean. Later, they would be gleaming in one of the stunning sunsets the area is famous for. We were lucky enough to get an outside seat in one of the lakeside restaurants and chatted and joked, sipping coffee, enjoying a Greek pastry, and watching the fishermen tending to their nets.

On the way back to the bus, we took a detour through the main shopping area of the town. As we strolled through the crowded streets, an elderly Greek lady who was passing by tripped on the pavement, the contents of her bags flying everywhere. Within the blink of an eye, Gabby was by her side, comforting and consoling. The lady obviously didn't understand a word but clearly picked up on the caring nature in the tone of her voice. I quickly refilled the bags, and then we both managed to get her back on her feet again. It was probably more embarrassing than painful for the dear woman, but she still gave Gabby a massive hug, babbling away in Greek. I realized I was 100 percent correct about what had drawn me to Gabby in the first place: she truly had a lovely heart and a very kind, gentle nature.

From there, we went on to the beach at Elounda, where we had free time before boarding the boat for Spinalonga Island. We discovered, quite by chance, a gyros kiosk and treated ourselves to some more incredibly delicious Greek food. The chicken was to die for, and it was served in pita bread and accompanied by tomatoes, onions, chips (fries), and a fabulous sauce called tzatziki.

It was a short journey out to the island, which had once been a home for the Venetians and Turks before becoming a leper colony. We walked all around, taking some fabulous photos in the superb weather. The highlight for me, however, turned out to be the swim stop on the way back, the boat anchoring off a beautifully scenic beach. The views were amazing—not just the beach, trees, and mountains in the distance, but also the incredibly clear, pristine, blue sea right in front of our eyes.

We were soon in that very sea, swimming together and dunking our heads underneath the beautiful water. That is, until Jinky decided to do a "bomber" right beside us, his arms clasped around his knees, resulting in a massive spray all around.

"How's it going, Jinks?" I ventured to ask.

"Cooling off, man, cooling off!"

"You need to cool off with Bertha, too," I ventured. "You could get into big trouble, you know, for what you did in the bus earlier. Think an apology would be in order, man."

"Yeah, I can't get that out of my mind. Must have had a really crazy night yesterday. Do you think she'll accept my apology?"

"You can try. You could even invite her out for a meal, Jinky," said Gabby.

"It'd never work," came his reply.

"You never know. It worked for me," responded Gabby. She turned her face and produced another one of those beautiful half-smiles I was becoming accustomed to (and liking very, very much).

Thankfully, the journey back was quiet and peaceful. Bertha had little more to add; and Jinky and Didge, who must have been drinking again, snored quietly in the back.

We had talked things over on the way out, and Gabby had agreed to have dinner at the hotel again after freshening up in the room. As we started on a delicious salad and a seafood main course, her phone rang. I could see a woman's picture on the screen. It was her mom, and she started talking in German.

"Hello, Mama . . . lovely to hear from you."

"Is it? You didn't say that two days ago."

"Sorry, Mom, I . . . I was in really bad form, really down."

"But today? You sound good. And there's a lot of background noise. Where are you?"

Just then, the waiter arrived with our drinks. "That's great, thank you very much," I said as I received them from him.

"Who is that, Gabriella? Who are you with?"

"It's a man I met yesterday, Mom. He's been through a lot recently as well. He's very kind and understanding."

"Gabby, I'd like to speak to your Mom," I interrupted.

"She doesn't speak English, Rob."

"No worries, pass me your phone, please. What's your surname, by the way?"

"It's Weber."

I immediately started speaking in Spanish. "Hello, Mrs. Weber. My name is Rob, a friend of Gabby's. She's very kindly agreed to have dinner with me. By the way, I hear you used to live in Madrid. Did you ever try the fried chorizo or the squid sandwich?"

"Yes, of course, delicious. It's just Hilda, by the way."

"Okay, Hilda. Incidentally, I've been trying to get Gabby to smile. You know, not just a smirk or a half smile. More like a full smile that spreads all over the face. Any ideas?"

The inevitable pause followed. It must run in the family, I thought.

"She's been through a really bad experience, Rob. Give her time."

"I will, Hilda. Lovely to talk to you. I'll pass you back to her. Bye for now."

I returned the phone to Gabby. Her mom immediately started talking again.

"Gabriella, who is he? I want to know everything about him."

"Mom, let me show you the food first. The buffet is amazing," Gabby replied before turning to me. "Just going inside to show Mom how it all looks, won't be long," she said to me as she headed back indoors.

Fifteen minutes later, she reappeared. It was the look in the eyes again that gave her away. Yesterday, I saw fear, worry, pain, hurt, anxiety. This time, I saw mischievousness—playfulness even. Or was it happiness?

"Well?" I asked her.

"Mom likes you."

"I like her, too. In fact, I really like her."

"Actually, she said the same. She really likes you, too. I think she's giving you credit for my change in mood. Said she can pick up happiness in my voice and face for the first time in ages. She also mentioned something about not forgetting to smile, that it's a bit of an obsession for you?"

"Never, did she really?" I replied, trying to bluff my way. However, my cheeks were not helping, rapidly changing to a bright red color, giving me away.

"You didn't tell me you speak Spanish, by the way," she went on, a smile forming on her face.

"Yeah, sorry, just didn't get around to it."

"I'd love to go with you tomorrow on the next tour, if that's okay?"

"Oh, that's fantastic. Thank you. It'll be another great day."

We chatted more about Hilda and her twin brother, Stefan, whom she'd spoken to as well. They seemed to be a very close-knit family, which I liked a lot. It reminded me of good, old Ireland.

"Eat up, Gabby. I want to show you the incredible views from the beach."

It seemed like the natural thing to do, to take her hand as we passed the floodlit swimming pool and gardens. Her small hand was lovely and warm to the touch. Even better, she didn't object or try to pull her hand away; and when I gave a gentle squeeze, she reciprocated in kind. We had almost arrived at the viewing point.

Dia Island stood out in the light of the full moon, the tips of the waves glistening in the hue of the water. The sea breeze made it colder than anticipated, so I did the gentlemanly thing, standing behind Gabby and pulling her into my body for warmth.

"Beautiful," I whispered in her ear. The beach? The waves? Dia Island? Gabby? Let her decide. She obviously chose the latter; for she turned round to face me, drawing closer and closer and catching me by surprise by giving me a kiss.

It was her turn now to whisper in my ear, "You said yesterday I was beautiful inside. What about the outside?"

Wow! What do you say to that? I chickened out with my answer. "I think it's time to get you home. Let's walk this way through the gardens for a change. We can get a taxi at the top."

She must have seen how red my face had become; but at least, I was rewarded with another half-smile on her departure, with yet more things to ponder over, especially as she'd agreed to accompany me for breakfast tomorrow morning, just before joining the day's trip.

CHAPTER 4
KNOSSOS PALACE

We arrived at the pick-up point at the front of the hotel in good time for the number one tour in all of Crete: a visit to Knossos Palace. We boarded the small minivan once more before transferring onto the larger bus at the foot of the mountains. Bertha was our guide again. Jinky and Didge were there as well, though they were seated further back in the bus!

It wasn't long before she was in full swing.

"Today you will have the pleasure of visiting the world-famous Knossos complex," she said. "You will explore the royal residence, including the Minoan king's throne, built during the Bronze Age. You will visit the House of the Frescoes to admire the colorful wall paintings. This tour is an absolute must-do on a visit to Crete; so well done, all of you, for coming along today. We always arrive early to avoid the lines; so on leaving the bus, you will pick up your audio headsets for the guided tour. Please follow me to the ticket kiosk; you can't miss my yellow umbrella. It is very hot today, and there is no protection from the sun; please put on plenty of sunscreen. There are toilets at the entrance just after the ticket office. For refreshments, there is a small café and veranda inside. As the palace is situated in quite a remote area, the only other refreshment place is the rather simple, run-down Greek tavern called Theos, located in the opposite direction from the ticket office . . . "

On arrival, we followed the yellow umbrella toward the ticket office, passing Jinky and Didge at the crossroads. They were obviously in a bit of a dilemma, about to make a very, very important decision.

"We've got the world-renowned Knossos Palace to our left, Didge, the number one tour in all of Crete. A must-do, according to big Bertha. Or we've got, to the right, the simple, run-down Greek tavern. Quite a difficult decision to have to make. What do you think, man? What should we do?"

The ruins were slightly disappointing, actually. Maybe this was because we'd both been to other places like Pompeii and the Colosseum in Rome. Maybe because the heat was somewhat overpowering, with no shade to be found anywhere. Or maybe it was due to the huge crowds that were swelling in number by the minute. We decided to leave the tour guide, give the ruins a once-over, and retire to Theos for some light refreshment. No surprise who we met on entering—Jinky and Didge.

"Hi, love birds, how was the Gnostic Temple?" asked Jinky, already a little tipsy.

"A little underwhelming, Jinky-with-a-J," I replied. "By the way, surely you can only spell Jinky with a J? Jinky with a G would be, like, Gin-ky? May be more appropriate?"

"It's Jinky with a J. Jinky with a J." His voice was back to that normal deep, loud tone.

"Okay, man, no worries. Jinky with a J it is."

Jinky fixed his eyes on Gabby before asking his next question. "You into dolphins,, babe?"

Gabby was wearing beautiful blue dolphin earrings which I'd noticed and admired earlier. Indeed, I was going to comment on how nice they looked when an opportunity arose. Trust him to beat me to it!

"I sure am Jinky. They're so cute and playful and love interacting with people, seemingly enjoying our company and admiration. Just like us, there're extremely intelligent and clever. You must have seen them jumping and splashing in their natural habitat?"

"Um no, can't say I have. Where're you from?" he replied, quickly changing the subject.

"I'm from Frankfurt, Jinky. Have you ever been there?"

"Yes, we have, actually—Didge and I, two years ago."

"No doubt you visited the world-famous Städel Museum with its fabulous art collection?"

"Eh? Not quite."

"Well, you must have been in the Römerberg, the historic market square? Everyone who comes to Frankfurt passes through it at least once. The timber houses, the cobbled streets, the Gothic church—sensational."

"Hmm. No, no."

"The Main Tower, the fourth tallest building in Germany? The views are amazing."

"No, listen. We did visit the Steiner Bar. It's famous for its Frankfurter sausages and stein beer. The lager just kept flowing and flowing all weekend. Pure paradise."

"Ah," said Gabby. "Of course."

"Hey, Jinky, ever been to the Riverside Stadium in Middlesbrough?" I asked. "I was there with a good friend, John Haley, to watch my team Chelsea take on the Boro. Very impressive stadium, and the fans were amazing as well."

"Where were you sitting then?" he asked somewhat doubtfully.

"If I remember correctly, it was the East Stand, low down, quite close to the pitch. But we were right beside the halfway line—fabulous views and only for £30, a bargain. I had to be careful, mind you, when Chelsea scored—couldn't celebrate too loudly, being surrounded by all those red and white scarves, including John, who is a Boro man through and through. It was a few years ago. Sadly, you didn't manage to stay up in the Premier League, which is a real pity for such a wonderful stadium and the incredible supporters you have."

"Yeah, we're loyal supporters all right, loyal to the core. No matter what division we're in."

It was time to escape and to find a table for ourselves.

Everyone made it back on time for the next part of the trip—a guided tour around Heraklion. However, as Gabby and I were taking another similar tour later on in the week, we decided instead to go our own way and have lunch in the highly rated Cori To restaurant. We definitely made the right choice, for the food was amazing: classic regional dishes bursting with flavor and taste. It certainly lived up to its billing: "Fresh food direct from our local farms; traditional Cretan food at its best." Everything was just that little bit classier, even the drinks! Soon, the conversation was flowing.

"You said you did the Inca Trail with Dave," Gabby said. "What's Peru like, Rob?"

"It's an amazing country, Gabby, and not just Machu Picchu. The city of Cusco is stunning, as is Arequipa, which is renowned for its beautiful historical center, a UNESCO World Cultural Heritage listing. It is also famed for having one of the most pleasant settings and climates in Peru. I heard the sun shines on 360 days of the year! Imagine that!

"But it's the backgrounds to these cities that I love, a bit like Edinburgh in Scotland, with the fabulous castle dominating the skyline. Arequipa is situated at the foot of an ice-capped volcano called El Misti, which is thankfully dormant! It is known as the "white city," as many of its colonial buildings are made of white ashlar or *sillar*, a volcanic stone extracted from El Misti or the two other neighboring volcanoes.

"And then you have Cusco, the former capital of the Incas, which stands at an altitude higher than eleven thousand feet, over two-and-a-half times the height of the UK's highest mountain, Ben Nevis. When we arrived directly from sea level, we had to lie down for a while to let our bodies become acclimated and build up red blood cells to avoid altitude sickness. The thin air makes it harder to breathe; but the rest did us a world of good, along with the hot herbal teas. Again, the city is surrounded by mountains, on three sides this time, providing that spectacular backdrop which can be seen from almost anywhere.

"There is the amazing culture, as well. Many agencies now place more emphasis on eco-tourism, taking their customers out into the local communities to experience the indigenous way of life: lifestyle, food, crafts, culture, etc. Yeah, and I really do have to plug the food. Did you know that Lima is the gastronomic capital of the Americas, having no less than a third of the top fifteen best Latin American restaurants in the world? I loved the *ceviche,* the raw fish, direct from the Pacific Ocean, marinated in lemon, lime, and other citric juices, accompanied by roasted corn, sweet potato, red onion, chili, and seasonings, such as garlic and coriander, served with a lettuce garnish."

"Hey, you're making me hungry again just listening to this!" she exclaimed.

"I haven't finished. In the provinces, as well, the food is outstanding. My favorite was a delicious soup called *caldo de gallina,* a tasty broth with lots of goodies added, such as hen, potatoes, chilies, noodles, and a boiled egg. The secret is to squeeze in some juice from the delicious small lemons they serve and dunk a slice of chili to give a touch of heat. And taste. *Oh que rico!* Fabulous. Delicious. And all washed down with, in my opinion, the best coffee in the world, the beans literally picked from the bushes in the jungle not far from Cusco. Yeah, it sure is some place. Sorry for ranting on a bit. What about you, Gabby? Got anything that tops Peru?"

"Well, yes, I think I do, although you'll probably cringe when you hear where our base was—Torremolinos! Yeah, it is a little past its best; but the hotel, the Melia Costa del Sol, was excellent, and the actual excursions from the town were amazing. My favorite was a day trip to Gibraltar, where we visited Europa Point, Saint Michael's Cave, and the Great Siege Tunnels. We even had time to take a cable car up to near the top of the rock. Actually, just as we reached the final station, a wild monkey landed on the roof, scaring the living daylights out of everyone! But to be able to see them up close was truly amazing. They looked cute yet are deadly; cuddly and tranquil—then, in an instant, violent and aggressive! During the Rock Tour, they landed on the roof of our minivan. The driver immediately stopped to let us all out to take some close-up pictures and videos. What an incredible experience!"

"Sounds amazing! What else did you do?" I asked.

"The caves at Nerja were really good as well. The Caminito del Rey trip was interesting: a two-and-a-half-hour hike through a narrow gorge, culminating with a rope bridge crossing, the bridge suspended more than three hundred feet above the ground. Spectacular views, as was true of the bridge at Ronda, high up in the mountains, set dramatically above another deep gorge, the bridge linking the old town to the new. Then, there was Granada and Alhambra as well. I could go on and on!"

Such were our times together, the conversation flowing non-stop, from one topic to the next, each taking turns to contribute and share. Everything seemed natural between the two of us. It was almost like we'd known each other for years, whereas it had only been two days! What a transformation had come over her since then. What a totally different person she was, her confidence and belief in herself fully restored.

However, it was now time to rejoin the tour party for the journey to Hersonissos and to my hotel. We just had time for a quick swim in the pool before dinner, both of us trying out the power waterslide, flying at top speed, whooping with delight and joy before crashing into the pool at the bottom, upside down.

Afterward, we spent a very relaxing evening together, enjoying a meal in the hotel's à la carte restaurant for a change. Then, disaster struck. When it was time for the desserts, which were self-service, I somehow got distracted and bumped into the massive three-tier cake stand on display at the side. Down I went onto the floor, with one of

ROBERT MARK WALKER   39

the tiers following right behind. Bumph! It landed plum on top of me, the cream and jam doing their best to make my face unrecognizable, apart from its rapidly reddening color! How embarrassing! But at least one good thing came out of it: I had fully completed my mission. Gabby was in fits of laughter; her face lit up with one of the widest, happiest smiles I had ever seen.

Later, Gabby decided to call Hilda and tell her all about the day. They chattered away excitedly, and her mom obviously picked up on Gabby's change as well; for when it was my turn to speak, the first thing she said to me in Spanish was, "Thank you very much, Rob!"

"For what, Hilda?" I replied.

"Gabby has been through a really bad time. As have I. As her mom, I have suffered along with her. I have felt her pain. I have cried when she cried. You have changed her, Rob, and I can't thank you enough for that. She seems to be having the time of her life. That's why I'm thanking you from the bottom of my heart. By the way, what about that smile you were after? She definitely must have done it. Tell me exactly how it happened. What did you say? Where were you? What were you doing? Tell me *everything!*"

"Eh?" I managed to get out. "What, Hilda?"

"You know, your challenge to get her to smile again? I want *all* the details."

"Um, I think that would be best coming from Gabby, Hilda. I'll pass you back over to her right away."

Within minutes, from what I could see on Gabby's phone, they were both rolling around in rapturous laughter. What's with women? Do they have to share everything? But I soon joined in, until the tears were running down our faces.

"I really like you, Rob," Hilda managed to get out.

"I really like you, too, Mamita."

All three of us chatted, laughed, and joked into the early hours of the morning before Gabby got a taxi home. I even managed to share a story about Dave with them, in Spanish and English.

"Dave is very good at his job and is one of the top salespeople for the clothing company he works for in Northern Ireland. It's run by a German company, and he was invited over to Munich to celebrate a special anniversary. Everyone of any importance was there, including the top directors from London. It was a very formal affair: dinner jacket, bow tie, the works. After a fabulous meal, it was time for the inevitable speeches and presentations, all the reps taking turns to introduce themselves. Two Germans went before Dave, each one standing up perfectly straight, clicking their heels, giving a deep bow, and saying, 'My name is Herr Adler from Berlin.' 'My name is Herr Ebert from Hamburg.' It was Dave's turn now, his bald head glistening in the heat of the room. Up he gets, fully erect, clicking his heels, bowing deeply, and saying, 'My name is No-hair Bloomer from Belfast, Northern Ireland!' Stunned silence, followed by a massive outburst of laughter and applause! That's the Bloom for you. He's so funny. Best friend ever."

CHAPTER 5
FREE TIME

It was originally planned to have a "chill" day halfway through the tour, a time to relax by the pool, try out the hotel's gym, tennis courts, etc. This worked out well for us: we were able to explore the beautiful coastline nearby, including the Saradari and Sarantari beaches. We passed an unofficial nude beach but decided to skip that! A superb brunch followed at the Pescado, a cute tavern located beside a small, quiet inlet. What a selection to choose from: octopus, shrimp, prawn skewers, catch of the day, fish soup, different types of bread with dips, and so much more! All washed down with glasses of ice-cold fruit juices, soft drinks, and water. The conversation, as usual, was also flowing.

"My Spanish isn't the best, Rob, but did I happen to hear you use the word *Mamita* last night when you were speaking to Mom?"

"Hmm. Maybe it just slipped out. She's such a lovely person. I really like her. You know what they say: like mother, like daughter!"

"Haha, I like that," said Gabby as she leaned over to give me a kiss. "And I really like you, too. Let's play a game of favorites, Rob. I'll go first. Favorite color?"

"Blue, as in Chelsea blue. Yours?"

"First choice, orange, as in the tints of the leaves at autumn or in the setting sun. Second choice, violet. Your turn."

"Favorite book?" I asked.

"I have a few, such as *Wuthering Heights* by Emily Brontë, considered by many to be one of the greatest romantic novels ever written. You?"

"This'll surprise you. It's a trilogy, actually, superbly written by Suzanne Collins—*The Hunger Games*."

"Oh, that's a bit violent and bloodthirsty."

"Yes, in parts, especially for the unfortunate kids chosen as tributes to fight to the death, with only one victor left standing at the end. But for me, the overall message is that dictators and injustice will never succeed. Against all the odds, the districts rise up and defeat the ruling government in Panem. But it's the way Collins has written the book—the plot and the pace, with everything interrelating. It is a masterpiece in storytelling. I must have read each one about ten times and still get a buzz!"

"Haha, you're funny. Favorite movie?"

"Again, this will probably surprise you. *Seven Pounds*, with Will Smith, Rosario Dawson, and Woody Harrelson. The title refers to the seven pounds of flesh that Will Smith's character, Ben, gives as a sort of payback for the seven innocent victims who died because of him. The acting is incredible. And I would be amazed if anyone could watch the ending with a dry eye and without shedding a bucketload of tears. I certainly couldn't, even though I've seen it five or six times. What about you?"

"Maybe it's my romantic nature again—I love Nicolas Spark's movies, such as *The Lucky One*, *The Last Song*, *Message in a Bottle*, and

The Choice. They're all brilliant, the screenplays incredibly well-written. I love them all. Okay, last one. Favorite vacation?"

"Peru or Portugal, hard to choose. I think, for the variety, I'll go for Portugal. Dave and I hired a car and had a few days in the Algarve getting a bit of a tan. We then moved on to Lisbon, which is an outstanding city. There's so much to see and do: the seven hills offer up fabulous views of the sea and metropolis; there are bustling markets, vibrant museums, castles, and towers. And, of course, a *pastel de nata* from any of the top bakeries was an absolute must! It was then further north up to Porto, which is a fabulous city as well, with beautiful bridges and a stunning old town, on the banks of the Douro River. Needless to say, we took a boat trip on the river, admiring the incredible views on either side. We enjoyed the local tapas, washed down with ice-cold fruit juices, refreshing in the summer heat. Others had green wine to drink—yes, I did say green!

"Anyway, next up was Braga, Guimarães, and the Gerês National Park. The park was sensational: we ended up swimming in mountain pools underneath a waterfall. You can imagine how refreshing that is, given that the temperature was around eighty-six degrees Fahrenheit. After all that, it was time for a delicious lunch served in a local restaurant. Our final stop was Évora before heading back to the airport at Faro. Your turn."

"Mom, Stefan, and I visited Dubrovnik in Southern Croatia. The old town is encircled by massive stone walls which you can walk around, with fabulous views of the Adriatic Sea. Good coffee as well, by the way! The tours were excellent, too; we chose the one-day trip to Montenegro, a visit to the Kravica Waterfall, and Mostar with its famous Old Bridge. We managed to find a place high up, looking down at the bridge from a height. Our guide had told us this was important if we wanted to appreciate the incredible blue colors of the river at its best and to get the most outstanding pictures. The interesting thing about the journey was having to cross into a narrow strip of land owned by Bosnia and Herzegovina, then back into Croatia again before entering Bosnia for a final time. Actually, they have just opened a new bridge, which makes it possible to bypass Bosnia and Herzegovina's short coastal strip at Neum. But the trip I liked best was the foodie tour, which included a visit to an oyster farm, tasting three-year-old oysters plucked directly from the sea. Pair that with freshly-squeezed lemon juice on top and homemade bread on the side—total perfection! From there, we were taken to a farmhouse for a typically rustic Croatian lunch. Delicious food, stunning scenery, and great company—what could be better!"

"What's still on your bucket list, somewhere you still really want to go to?" I asked.

"I think that would have to be Dubai, when I can afford it. I've heard a great deal about the place. Yeah, it's definitely Dubai."

"Gabby, do you believe in God?" I suddenly blurted out. Out of all the questions I had asked, this was, by far, the one I was really concerned about.

"Yes, I do, Rob. I actually made a commitment at a Christian summer camp one time, but things sort of fizzled out after that. I sense it means a lot to you?"

"It does, Gabby. It really does. What about you? What made it fizzle out?"

"Doubts. Disillusionment. Everything going against us. Things like that."

Already I could read her like an open book. There was a lot more under the surface she wasn't telling me. But a prompting inside made me leave it at that. I decided to change the subject.

"How about some pool time to chill out, relax, and have a swim?"

"Sounds great; let's go!"

It was such a pleasure and joy to spend time with Gabby, the conversation spontaneous and unforced. It continued on the walk back to the hotel. We both settled down for a quieter time of reading and sunbathing by the pool. But even these moments felt natural, like we didn't have to be talking to each other all the time. Then, it was time for a swim to cool off. Eventually, one of the event organizers came around inviting everyone to the pool aerobics. While Gabby joined in the dancing and moving to the Latino rhythm in the shallow end of the pool, I had a workout in the gym.

Afterward, as we sat having dessert on the veranda, Gabby's phone rang. It was her mom, and she was obviously distressed. "Excuse me, Rob. I'd better take it by the pool," Gabby said. It was half an hour later when she returned; and I could tell something was wrong, as her eyes were brimming with tears.

"Come on, Gabby, let's go," I said gently. Taking her by the hand, I led her back to the room. Once inside, she immediately threw herself into my arms and burst into tears. She was hurting, and now I was as well.

"Let it all out, babe. Just let it all out," I said, rubbing her back at the same time. We didn't say anything as the tears and sobs continued. I knew only too well from my past the importance of waiting in a time like this. She would tell me what had happened when she was ready.

"I've never told you about Dad. He was killed four years ago as he was walking across a pedestrian crossing. The driver was driving a red Ferrari F8. He was speeding and failed to stop. Thankfully, a witness took note of the license plate number, and the police arrested him shortly after. Twenty years old, three times over the alcohol limit. Dad died at the scene. The man, Menzel, was jailed for six years. Apparently, he went out of his way to impress the parole board. He managed to get out after three years. He was released today.

"Our lawyer has just been on the phone with Mom. She apologizes for having to interrupt our holiday and hopes not to spoil it. But she was desperate, Rob. She couldn't tell Stefan. They were very close: Dad took him to all the Eintracht Frankfurt home games. He never missed any of Stefan's games, either, when he played in goal for his local high school team. Both of Mom's parents have passed on, and my poor grandparents on Dad's side are heartbroken to this day. I'm really, really close to Mom, hence her call. She had to share her feelings with someone."

"Gabby, there is no need to apologize. She must be devastated. You, too. I'm heartbroken for you all," I replied.

"Do you know what the worst thing for us was at the trial? Menzel showed no remorse whatsoever. He even smiled at me, flirting. His family is pretty wealthy, apparently, so no doubt, they had the best lawyers available. Six years. Well, three years, actually. Where's the justice in that, Rob? It's just not right. It's not fair. Our hearts are broken. The pain never goes away; the grief is always there, every single day of our lives. We will never get over it. Dad will not be at my wedding; to walk me down the aisle; to play with my children; to hug, support, and encourage me. To love me. Never, ever. I miss him deeply."

The tears continued to flow, her body shaking, the sobbing endless. She was right, of course. Grief never gets any easier to bear. It's the victims and their friends and loved ones who suffer, who never forget, who are left hurting every single day of their lives. They're the ones who so often have nightmares and find sleep hard to come by, who feel lonely and depressed, who try to keep on going, carrying their pain and burdens through the "death zone," come what may. They're the ones who feel let down by the so-called justice system—while Menzel moves on, without remorse, without a care, without pity, to live his life happily ever after. Where is the honesty in that? The fairness? The justice?

I felt my throat tighten up. I, too, was heartbroken. Her grief was my grief; her pain, my pain; her loss, my loss. She was still in my arms, taking comfort from the close contact.

I felt the need to console her more. "I once visited a place called Ayr in Scotland. It's a popular seaside resort, with beautiful walks along the esplanade and sandy beach, which offers up fabulous views of the Isle of Arran. This quaint little island, often called 'Scotland in Miniature,' stands out from its surroundings, the mountains resplendent in the sunshine during the day or gleaming in the stunning sunsets the area is famous for. But this is not always the case; and on that day, all I could see was a thick, cold, dense fog, known locally in Scotland as a *haar*. Apparently, this is a common occurrence on certain days during spring and summer, when the island seems to disappear, becoming invisible due to the fog. But despite not being able to see the island, I knew it was still there, that I would be a fool to say it no longer existed.

"It's a bit like that for me, Gabby, with Julie. I can't see her; she's invisible to me. Yet she's still there, looking down on me, supporting me, egging me on, her presence and touch on my life always here, always present, always out there, even when it doesn't appear so. In one way, she still exists. She still—in some unknown way—supports, encourages, and loves me and will always be part of my life and everything I do. But I need to keep on going. I must never give up. I must have faith, right to the end. And so must you.

"You've probably gathered by now that I'm a Christian. My faith keeps me going, Gabby—all the promises in the Bible, God's presence and touch upon my life. Faith is the fuel of the Christian life, making us certain of all these things. It is often difficult to see through the fog of this world and beyond the challenges and hardships life throws at us. But we must go on, never giving up. We must believe that God is always there, always present, always out there, even when it doesn't appear so. No matter what we are going through, no matter what crisis we are experiencing, we are never, ever alone."

She sat in silence for a moment, but I could tell she was not happy. As the seconds passed, her face changed, becoming redder and redder. Her next words were said almost through clenched teeth.

"Where was He when Dad died? Where was He then, Rob? Why didn't He prevent it happening? If Dad had arrived five seconds earlier or later he would still be here today. Five seconds, was that too much to expect? I had made a commitment to God, and He had let this happen. You asked me before what made it fizzle out. Well, that's my answer, along with you pushy people with all your sweet talk. Sorry, that last bit was uncalled for. Thank you for today, Rob. I'm tired. I'm going to sleep in tomorrow. I'll make my own way home. Good night."

Then, in the blink of an eye, she was gone. There was almost total silence on the outside, apart from the sound of the breeze blowing in from the Aegean Sea. But inside, my heart was racing, like a hummingbird's wings. How had it all gone so wrong? I thought my arms wrapped around her had brought comfort and solace; arms of protection, a bit like the walls around Dubrovnik that Gabby had mentioned, providing shelter against the sea, rains and invading armies. I thought my words had brought encouragement and consolation, hope and belief. Anything but. It was time to get out into that fresh air to clear my mind, to walk and to talk to God. Then it was time for bed.

I thought it was the alarm that woke me early the next morning but I was mistaken. My phone was ringing, and it was a number I didn't recognize.

"Hello?" I managed to ask, after almost sending it flying from the table by mistake. I recognized the voice, though, her Spanish crisp, fluent, and precise.

"Rob, Gabby's not smiling again. She's quite upset. Actually, not so much with you, though. She thinks she overreacted last night."

"Oh, Hilda! Oh, Hilda! God is good! Sorry . . . sorry. Thank you. Do you think I should call her?"

"No, definitely not! I think you should go to her hotel right now and open your arms wide!"

"Hilda, thank you! Thank you so much. Would you happen to know her room number? Thanks. I'm on my way now!"

And so I was, after a quick change and visit to the restroom. It was still early when I arrived and knocked on the door.

"Who is it?" I think she said, but then again, my German's not the best.

I sent an arrow prayer up to Heaven, breathed deeply, and said just one word: "Rob." The wait seemed interminable; but eventually, the door creaked open. She stood there in front of me, expressionless, silent, and hard to read.

"Gabs, I'm sorry about last night. I don't apologize for what I said; my faith means everything to me. But so do you. I . . . I . . . "

I should have listened to Hilda and simply opened my arms wide! It wasn't necessary, though, for it was Gabby who opened hers, running toward me! The words were flowing—tears, too, for that matter—as we hugged each other tightly. But these were tears of joy—and love. I was now certain of two things, 100 percent clear. The first was that I was here for Gabby, here to help, to hug, to support, and to encourage. I would be with her through these horrible times and memories of distress and despair. And the second was this: I knew, without any doubt that I was falling in love with this girl.

CHAPTER 6
GRAMVOUSA ISLAND AND BALOS LAGOON

T hankfully, we made it on to the bus in time for the three-hour journey to the port of Kissamos, in the westernmost part of Crete. Gabby seemed to have recovered from the last night and was her usual joking self.

"You called me *babe* last night for the first time," she purred in my ear. "Kind of like it."

"I kinda like you, too," came my reply.

We kissed and cuddled in together, the heat of our bodies helping us to doze off.

From the port, it was a short boat ride over to the Balos Lagoon, renowned for its golden sands and crystal-clear water. What a joy to relax on the beach, warming our bodies in the glorious sunshine before cooling off in that calm, inviting sea. As we relaxed and enjoyed ourselves, the crew prepared a rustic lunch for those willing to pay a little extra. There is something special about eating out in the open air with all those incredible views and the sun and light sea breeze on our backs. Was it this that made the food taste all the better? Or was it just the fact that Greek food is delicious, full stop?

Next up was Gramvousa, also known as "Pirate's Island," with over one hundred bird and four hundred plant species. We spotted some amazing-looking vultures and eagles up on the higher ridges. But it was the Venetian castle that proved to be the big attraction here. The panoramic views from the rocky hill left us speechless, the sun reflecting off the deep blue waters of the Aegean Sea. Sea turtles and dolphins played in the water on the return to Kissamos.

"Look at those beauties!" exclaimed Gabby, pointing her finger in obvious delight and excitement at the dolphins. "They're having such fun jumping and frolicking in the water. I think they're smiling at us!"

"Just like me Gabby," I replied, looking into her lovely face. "I've just realized that's a great name for a fishing port, "Kiss we must!"

"Haha," she responded with her usual enthusiasm. "Let's do it then!"

On the return bus journey, we again snuggled in close together, feeling tremendous comfort, companionship, and consolation—both from our physical proximity and from a sense of a peaceful wholeness and harmony from within. These were feelings and sensations I hadn't experienced for some time now. I felt good again, happy, content, satisfied. Things were looking up. Life was good. I looked at the beautiful girl curled up beside me in the seat, who was now dozing peacefully, happily dreaming, and realized once again that she was the reason for it all.

"You're truly beautiful," I whispered quietly. This was more for me to hear, a confirmation of completeness, of perfection. There was a flawlessness in our relationship, an exquisiteness and excellence way beyond anything I had ever experienced. I had to smile. I had to very gently touch her, stroking her face. And I had to, no matter what, do everything in my control, everything possible, to cling to these feelings endlessly, forever and ever.

Back at the hotel, a special International Talent Night had been organized for all the guests. It was an outside buffet this time, the barbecues working non-stop, disgorging huge amounts of steaks, seafood, ribs, chicken, and pulled pork, along with the vegetarian and vegan options. There was quite a representation of countries participating in the evening's entertainment, as well as plenty of variety. The highlight for us was a sketch by a family from South Korea called the Hans. The two parents appeared on stage, along with their two teenage sons. They must have rigged the drawing, as the eldest boy's name, Samuel, came out of the hat; and he had to take part in a version of "Blind Date." The three teenage girls, who had obviously agreed beforehand to take part, were behind a screen on stage, out of Samuel's view. They then answered his questions, with a lot of gusto and enthusiasm.

As the questions progressed, everyone could see how excited he was becoming. Finally, he chose girl number three. At the very last minute, girl number three was replaced by Samuel's mom! When the screen was pulled back, the poor lad's face told it all. He had been totally fooled! The audience exploded into laughter and rapturous applause.

Finally, Gabby's goading got the better of me, so up I went on stage to sing a lovely Irish ballad or melody called "The Boys from County Armagh." The secret was to involve everyone in the chorus, singing along with me. I hadn't planned it; but when they all started swaying from side to side in perfect rhythm, I knew it had been a success. Oh, and of course, Gabby's massive grin, hug, and kiss gave further confirmation!

As we had another early start the next day, Gabby returned to her hotel as soon as the entertainment was over. Needless to say, the Hans were called back on stage to win the prize for the best presentation of the evening.

CHAPTER 7
SAMARIA GORGE

I t was a 6:00 a.m. pick-up, the earliest to date. Still, we were soon snuggled in together, the warmth of the bus and our bodies making for a very pleasant journey to our first stop at Rethymno again, this time for breakfast.

Next up was the famous plateau Omalos, a tableland surrounded by the Lefka Ori (White Mountains), which, unfortunately, were now bare of their picturesque snow cover, due to the summer weather. Nevertheless, the views were still striking, and we could see our destination not far ahead.

The Samaria Gorge, the longest in Europe, is one of the most spectacular treks in Crete. At almost ten miles of uneven, rocky terrain in length and taking between four to six hours to complete, it is a challenging hike, definitely not one for beginners. But both Gabby and I were well-seasoned hikers, Gabby having explored the Taunus mountain range north of Frankfurt and I having climbed Ben Nevis on two different occasions (the first one with the Scouts when I was twelve years old).

However, just before setting off from Xyloskalo, the entrance to the national park, our party found itself with two extra persons. The ticket controller was not amused, and our guide proceeded to take a roll call.

"Adair?"

"Present."

"Blair?"

"Yo!"

"Degenhardt?"

"Here."

"Fuller?"

"Bingo!"

Just then, two people came forward, apologized, and started to leave.

"Shame!" said "Bingo" man. (There's always one!)

We followed the path along the route of the ancient Taras River and were soon mesmerized by the beauty of the Cretan wilderness in its purest form. The scenery was stunning, both of us agreeing that it was some of the best we had ever seen. We decided to take our time, stopping often to take pictures, to have a snack, to refill our water bottles from the fresh mountain streams and mini-cascades, to try and get close (no luck) to the wild cliff goats (known as kri-kri), and to explore the ancient caves that had provided shelter during times of war and were now home to the goats. There was also an abandoned village to look at before arriving at the so-called "Iron Gates," almost two miles from the end of the trek. The gates are actually a very narrow thirteen-foot-wide section of the gorge, with one-thousand-foot-tall cliffs on either side—very impressive, indeed.

We finally arrived at the beautiful, isolated fishing village called Agia Roumeli, nestled between huge rocks and the expansive Libyan

Sea. It was time for a refreshing swim in that very sea, followed by lunch in a local tavern.

We shared a table with an Italian couple who were very welcoming and chatty. As I looked at Gabby, engrossed in the conversation, a smile constantly on her face, I thought back to another table shared only five days ago. How far had I gotten with my list of objectives since then? Get a smile out of her? Check. A change of mood? Check. A lightening of the spirit? Check. A touch of joy? Yep, success all around. But what about me? Smiling more? Definitely. Less moody? For sure. An enlightened spirit? Absolutely! A fun vacation? The best ever! It had been a great adventure today, just like every other day on this amazing break.

"What?" She had just caught me smiling and staring at her.

I leaned over and gave her a long, passionate kiss, oblivious to the Italians, to the other tourists, and to the rest of the world.

On the scenic boat ride back to the bus at Sfakia, I asked her which gorge she had liked more, today's hike or the Caminito Del Rey in Spain.

"They were both quite different, really. The Samaria Gorge was certainly much more rustic and over twice as long to complete, though with a lot fewer people. I enjoyed the swim and the refreshments in the tavern at the end of today's trek. I think the scenery was nicer here, too. And the company certainly was!"

That massive, beautiful smile spread all across her face once again as I took her hand in mine and kissed it tenderly.

We had one final, delightful surprise still to come: a final stop to try some delicious souvlaki, grilled and served in an attractive outdoor garden. We wolfed down skewer after skewer of mouth-watering, tender grilled meats and vegetables, served with pita bread, lemons, sauces, and fries. What a wonderful way to end the perfect day.

CHAPTER 8
FOOD AND WINE TOUR

How do you tell someone that you love them? When on earth is the right time to express that love, to pluck up the courage and spill it all out? What if they don't feel the same way? What if they don't reciprocate in an affirmative way? I was doubting myself and delaying. My thoughts and prayers were obviously on Gabby, thinking about her, mulling over the previous six days. For I knew now, as much as I'd ever been certain about anything in my whole life, that I loved her; and I loved her deeply. I wanted this to go on, to develop further into something much, much more than a summer romance.

But what about Gabby? I knew she liked me. I knew she was such a changed person from our first encounter at Preveli Beach. I knew that she, too, was enjoying every single minute of our time together. But did she love me? This was the big question. There was a twelve-year age difference between us. I had been married before. I was a Christian. Would these things be playing on her mind? She'd also just been through a horrendous experience with someone who said he loved her. But his words had been shallow and hollow; he had no idea of the meaning of love, of the commitment involved, of the need to please and to give, to compromise wherever possible. He was all take, take, take. What should I do?

My thoughts suddenly flickered to a past vacation in Aviemore, in the Scottish Highlands. It's a popular vacation resort in the Cairngorms, surrounded by towering mountains and sparkling lochs. The air is as fresh as it gets! It is a home to stunning scenery and wonderful wildlife. It is also the home to the Landmark Forest Adventure Park, which I once visited during the Easter holidays. There are many activities going on, from the Runaway Timber Train to the Wild Water Coaster, from the Tree Top Trail to the Fire Tower, which, as the UK's tallest wooden tower, offers amazing views.

The highlight for me turned out to be the Sky Dive, described in the brochure as "beyond white knuckle, the ultimate dare, the ultimate achievement." It is basically a forty-five-foot pole or log which people step off and, by means of a harness, land gently on the ground. I watched a young girl try to do it. Her family coaxed her. I coaxed her. The cable operator beside her coaxed her. Instead of standing up, she tried sitting down, hoping to just slide off. Nothing worked. Her face was contorted with fear. What do you think the harness operator did next? He crept up behind her and pushed her off! Within a second or two, the cable cut in; and she glided gently to the ground. Then, after all the cheering and clapping, the biggest smile we'd ever seen flashed across her face!

Surely, it couldn't be that hard to do? I decided to have a go myself. I climbed up the ladder, put the harness on, walked across the ledge, and looked down. Utter fear ran through me. From the ground, forty-five feet looks like nothing; and the pole seemed relatively small. But from up there, it was a totally different story. Thoughts of climbing back down entered my head. I tried to jump off one side, which didn't work. Finally, I plucked up the courage, stepped off, and with legs kicking everywhere in mid-air in panic, landed on the ground. My heart was thumping.

The instructor shouted down, "It's that step of faith, isn't it?"

Just like the harness and cable, which allowed for a safe descent and gentle landing from the Sky Dive, so, too, I realized, God's almighty hand was upon me: upholding and helping me to overcome, ever present with me in every trial and difficulty I met in life. Phrases from the Bible, such as "mighty hand" and "strong hand," came to mind. I remembered the incredible story of the parting of the Red Sea, how the Israelites were able to walk across on dry land, with walls of water on every side.[1] The Lord brought them out. The Lord rescued them. The Lord was with His people, fulfilling every promise He had made to them. And His people were victorious!

I immediately felt reassured. That despite the seriousness of the situation we are going through, no matter how difficult the problem may appear to be, to God, it is nothing. With His help, with His strong hand, we, too, can overcome. He makes our steps firm; though we stumble, we will not fall; "the LORD upholds [us] with his hand."[2] We have to believe this! We need to claim wholeheartedly the wonderful promises the Bible contains. We are required to never doubt or have unbelief.[3] Instead, we are called to have tenacious faith, clinging firmly to the great hope the Gospel brings. And it is also necessary to put this faith into practice. We sometimes need to step off the ledge, taking that step of faith. The cable only functions when the person actually steps off the platform. God desires us to take that step of faith.

---

1   Exodus 14:22.
2   Psalm 37:23-24.
3   Hebrews 3:19.

I now realized that I had to pluck up the courage and express my feelings to Gabby. I had to remove any doubt from my mind and delay no longer. It was time to trust in God and step off that log once again. Our penultimate trip was the food and wine tour in Heraklion, Crete's capital, which ran from 12:00 p.m. to 4:00 p.m. Heraklion is a port city with an attractive harbor guarded by a beautiful Venetian fortress. The city is the fourth largest in the whole of Greece and is always buzzing with tourists and locals alike. We arrived at the prearranged meet-up point in good time and were introduced to our guide, Amelia, and four other people, two couples from the USA. It was fascinating to listen to Amelia explaining all about the island's culinary culture as we wandered through local neighborhoods, away from the beaten track. What a joy to sample authentic Cretan delicacies.

Our first stop set the tone, a fabulous family-owned business whose speciality was bougatsa, washed down with the inevitable cup(s) of Greek coffee. This mainly sweet, filo-type breakfast pastry, made from semolina custard and cheese (or minced meat), literally melted in the mouth. The filling is covered in layers of phyllo (filo), a very thin unleavened dough, the same as that used to make baklava. This is then brushed with oil or butter and placed in the oven. Our guide had to order double portions all around; it really was that good!

From there, we entered the local market and had a very interesting talk about the products on offer: the famous olives, rusks, and local cheeses, all of which we got to taste. Amelia had her own small olive orchard (or grove) and went on to explain that, due to the very warm climate, lack of air pollution, and strict care and pressing regulations,

Cretan oils are some of the finest in the world, particularly noted for their high polyphenol content and low acidity levels. We couldn't have agreed more, as we dipped the cheese, rusks, tomatoes, and other goodies into small bowls of pure organic virgin olive oil. Fabulous! Next stop was another long-established family business famous for its organic meat dishes, such as apáki (smoked and cured pork loin) and a delicious casserole dish called tsigariastó. Unfortunately, there was no goat on the menu this time around—I had tasted that delicacy previously on another Greek island called Zante and absolutely loved it. However, the apáki and tsigariastó were good substitutes; and again, we almost licked the plates clean!

As we walked from tasting to tasting, Amelia highlighted all the major sights, giving us a run-down on the city's history at the same time. She told us with some pride how, during the Cretan War, the Ottomans besieged the city for twenty-one years, from 1648 to 1669, the longest siege in history up until that time. The local populace refused to give in, and the city was only lost after betrayal from within. How on earth could they resist for twenty-one years with little food or water? The tremendous fighting spirit of the wonderful Greek people shone through in this fascinating history lecture.

It was time for our final stop and a chance to taste a glass of some delicious, ice-cold fruit juice. Grape growing in Crete has a long history, dating back to the Minoans during the Bronze Age. As we sipped our drinks, the conversation flowed. The two couples (both married)—Charlotte and Ryan from Hartford, Connecticut, and Harris and Debbie from Dallas, Texas—were great fun. Debbie was quite a stunner, actually, her hazel-colored eyes and dark brown skin resplendent in the sunshine. Harris was a very lucky guy!

"Hey, guys, did you know Charlotte is a soccer referee?" asked Ryan.

"Shush, Ryan, not everyone's into soccer, you know."

"Well, I only have to say one thing more," he added. "She's just received an invitation from the English Football Association to referee games in the English Championship. Quite an honor, huh?"

"Wow, that really is impressive," I said. "Well done, you. I once had to stand in to referee a game at short notice. Just couldn't believe my friends. Once that whistle was in my hand, in their eyes I was a totally different person: no longer a friend or someone they knew really well. It was all 'Hey, ref!' or 'Come on, ref, that was a clear foul!' Don't envy you, Charlotte, but good on you."

"Charlotte, we just met two big, fanatical Middlesbrough supporters here in Crete. I don't envy you either; they're sure to give you some trouble," said Gabby.

"Oh, I'm used to that. And don't worry, I know how to handle guys like that."

"Been to see any Premier League matches, Ryan?" I asked. "The soccer is amazing."

"I have, actually, Rob. Went to see Chelsea play about a year ago. It was a fabulous game against Aston Villa, Chelsea winning three to one."

"Then, as a Chelsea fan, you're not going to believe this," I added. "The only way my best friend Dave and I could get tickets to see the Blues was through hospitality. So, we decided to make a weekend out of it. Well, there we were, the night before the match, strolling back to the Chelsea FC Millennium Hotel, when we suddenly noticed Eden Hazard and N'Golo Kanté in a little area off to the side. Let me get it on my phone—my favorite selfies ever! There you go. Yeah, this was obviously when Hazard was still at Chelsea. The players had parked their cars in the hotel's underground car garage and were en route to a private training ground and hotel not far from the Bridge. So, they were totally relaxed, in no rush whatsoever, waiting for the rest of the squad and quite happy to chat away with us. Get this, there were only three other fans alongside us. It was one of those moments of a lifetime, a chance encounter never to be forgotten and probably never, ever to be repeated. We were both ecstatic."

"I think I've got one almost as good," said Harris. "I was over on a business trip to the UK, and we managed to take time out to visit Saint Andrews in Scotland. It was a joy to explore the medieval center of narrow alleys, cobbled streets, and ancient ruins, as well as the nearby fishing settlements of Saint Monans, Pittenweem, Anstruther, and, my favorite, the village of Crail. But of course, we were there chiefly to have a game at the Home of Golf, on the famous links course. And who should we bump into but Jack Nicklaus and Tom Watson having a practice round before the Senior Open Championship event. Fate or what? Awesome. Great guys and ever so friendly. And speaking of selfies, take a look at this one!"

Just then, Amelia rose to say her goodbyes. "Listen everyone, sorry to interrupt, but I'm afraid I'm going to have to love you and leave you. My family will be expecting dinner on the table soon. You've been a wonderful group. If you pop in a favorable review about today's tour, that would be appreciated. Enjoy the rest of your time in Crete."

We all said our farewells, each giving her a well-deserved tip. She had gone out of her way to show us all the major sights and had been more than excellent.

After she left, Charlotte took over. "Okay, guys, when we meet as couples like this, I always like to find out how we all met up. Okay? So, I'll go first." She wasn't having no for an answer!

"Ryan and I have similar interests," she continued. "We love sports. We love music and dancing. We love the mountains—camping, hiking, climbing. We love adventure. So, a mutual friend of ours, Katy, did a little bit of matchmaking. She set us up on a blind date and, man, did we hit it off right from day one. Right, babe?"

"Spot on," said Ryan. "I've been indebted to Katy ever since. What a find!" He took her hand in his; and the inevitable kiss followed, accompanied by our "oohs" and "aahs."

"What about you guys?" Charlotte asked Debbie and Harris.

It was Harris who answered. "We've been friends ever since preschool. Our families grew up together. We grew up together, attending the same church. It was no surprise to anyone when I asked Debs out. Or when we got engaged. Or when we married. It seemed like the natural thing to do. And I've never regretted one moment of it."

"Me neither," echoed Debbie as they kissed, and we "oohed" and "aahed" again.

"Your turn, guys."

I looked at Gabby, who gave an affirmative nod.

"I want you to tell me what your take on this is, okay?" I started. "We first met on the beach. There was only one spot left, which I was rushing to get. She beat me to it by seconds, and I had to go elsewhere. About two hours later, I arrived for lunch at the only restaurant in the place. It was packed to the rafters. There was only one little table left with one empty seat. The other was occupied by Gabby, and I sat down beside her."

"Oh, my goodness," said Charlotte. "That's how you met? What a coincidence! What are the chances of that happening?"

"More like luck?" chipped in Ryan.

"Or fate. Or, like you guys said, another chance encounter," added Harris.

"No, no. I think it was more than that. I think it was planned," said Debbie.

"What do you mean, Debs?" asked her husband.

"You know, angels. A Divine, heavenly touch, almost?"

"Hmm, interesting," added Harris.

"I think it was love, that we were destined to be together," said a voice roughly where Gabby was sitting. I couldn't believe what I had just heard. I looked at her. She was biting her bottom lip. Then, she looked at me right in the eyes—her pupils enormous, a bit like the cute cat, Puss in Boots, in *Shrek 2*—and gave me one of those incredibly beautiful smiles of hers. That's when I lost it. I literally shot up from the chair and jumped into her arms. The other two couples had kissed each other as well, but this was at a different level—the passion flowing, the intensity and prolonging of the kiss, the hunger and desire. It was as if the others weren't present; it was just the two of us, wrapped in each other's arms, in our own little world.

"I think it was love, that we were destined to be together," she had said, and I knew she was partially right, for I was in total agreement with Debbie. We *were* meant to be together because God had planned it right from the start and because love had developed out of our coming together. The four words popped out of my mouth naturally, without any thought or hesitation whatsoever. "I love you, Gabs."

"I love you, too, Rob."

And then, the dam burst, tears flowing down our faces like a river in full flow. We clung to each other, whispering words of love, of fondness, of tenderness and deep affection, uncaring who else might hear, who else might be watching, our pent-up feelings and desires finally being released. This was love in its purest form.

When we eventually sat down again, it was Charlotte who spoke first. "Wow, guys, that was awesome! That was truly awesome. I've never, ever had a reaction like that to my question. Thank you, Gabby and Rob, for . . . for sharing your love with us, for making our day!"

"So, when did this encounter happen?" asked Ryan. It was my turn to nod to Gabby.

"Six days ago," she purred.

"What!" exclaimed Harris. "Aw, that is beautiful. I think we're all going to cry! Please, tell us more. Tell us everything!"

We told it all but left out the personal stuff about our hurts and losses; that was for Gabby and me alone, and our families, and Dave and Jacqui. The 4:00 p.m. finish time was long gone as we chatted, giggled, and laughed well into the evening before taking taxis back to our respective hotels. What a day! What a night! What a girl! I was totally head over heels in love!

CHAPTER 9
DIA ISLAND

It was another glorious day as we snuggled together in the taxi, relaxing in each other's arms, chatting about the day before, kissing and cuddling and continuing to express our love. We had even managed to update Hilda and my parents on the past few days' events. Mom and Dad in Ireland had been both surprised and delighted when I introduced them to Gabby. They took to her straight away and, of course, invited her over to Armagh, our hometown. Truth be told, they had been very worried about me during these past two very difficult years and saw Gabby as an answer to their prayers.

For today, I had booked the late afternoon catamaran cruise to Dia Island, the beautiful little uninhabited isle we had seen often from the hotel. It had actually been quite tricky arranging the itinerary: some tours operated on Tuesdays and Thursdays only, others on Fridays and Mondays, and so on. This trip ran every day, so it was the very last to be slotted in on whatever day was still available. Call it a coincidence or whatever, but it turned out to be the perfect time for us to take the cruise: our last full day together in Crete. Whereas yesterday was all about socializing and mixing with Charlotte, Ryan, Debbie, Harris, and even Amelia, which we enjoyed immensely, today was just about the two of us, in the romantic setting of one of the most picturesque islands and bays in the area.

The catamaran departed at 3:00 p.m. from Heraklion Marina, so we had plenty of time beforehand for soft drinks and a light brunch in a delightful outdoor restaurant overlooking both the harbor and the Venetian fortress. Suddenly, two guys we were beginning to get to know really well came strolling past, looking absolutely miserable. It was Jinky and Didge. Their misery was due to a lack of funds—they too were due to fly home tomorrow but had totally run out of money.

"Hey, Jinky, Didge," I called out. "How's it going? Come over and join us." As they approached, I said, "We have to leave in half an hour, guys, but sit down and tell us what you've been up to."

While they started to do this, I managed to get the waiter's attention and ordered food and drinks for them.

"Hey, guys, what's up with your faces? They're so red," Gabby politely interrupted with considerable concern.

"Red as a lobster, babe," replied Jinky.

"Or as a beetroot!"

"Or as a tomato!"

Their mood was clearly changing for the better.

"Right, you obviously haven't been using any suntan lotion at all in this hot weather. Thankfully, I always have a small emergency bottle of aloe vera handy, so I'll pop some gel on your faces right now."

"Oh, that's cold, babe, but really good. Thank you," crooned Jinky.

"So, what have you guys been up to since we last met?" I eventually asked.

"Just chilling at the hotel in the resort. It's all-inclusive, which is great. Free beer and grub. Oh, and we bumped into Bertha again, and yes, I apologized to her. It cost me more than a drink, mind you—had to buy her a pizza as well."

"Ah. She's got such a big heart to forgive you," said Gabby.

"Yeah, she sure has. I'm slowly learning, guys; and believe it or not, I quite fancy her. We got along really well together, and she's genuinely quite funny—not all serious, solemn, and sedate like I thought she would be. She's actually lovely inside and has a great personality. She made me laugh. I've even got her phone number!"

"Good for you. You're learning, man. It's the inside that counts," I said as I caught Gabby's eye and gave her a wink and a massive smile.

"We finally won a prize at the three penalties competition," chipped in Didge. "It was easy to score the first two. The last one was always the hard one. We had a ball, though, if you pardon the pun."

"I've got a question for you two," I said. "Where was the penalty kick invented?"

"That's easy. Definitely England, where soccer was invented," replied Jinky immediately.

"You, Didge?" I asked.

"Same."

"Both wrong. I come from the city of Armagh in Northern Ireland. My mom was brought up in a little village called Milford, two miles outside the city. In those days, it had a population of less than a thousand. That was where it was invented."

"Rubbish. No way, man, you're making that up," said Jinky.

"Honestly. It was credited to a goalkeeper and businessman named William McCrum in 1890. As a member of the Irish Football Association, he proposed that a penalty kick should be awarded to stop defenders from hacking down the opposition players in order to prevent them from scoring. There's even a commemorative plaque and bust in his honor in the village to this day. Look it up on Google."

"Hey, guys, want to hear a good soccer gag?" This was Gabby. "Who would you say are Middlesbrough's main soccer rivals?"

"We have lots of rivals but primarily three," replied Jinky. "Sunderland, Sunderland, and Sunderland! No, just kidding, Sunderland, Newcastle, and Leeds."

"Okay, let's go for Sunderland, then. My brother, Stefan, told me this joke. He's an Eintracht Frankfurt fanatic. There's a little rivalry to this day between our team, the Eagles, and FC Kaiserslautern. So, I'm going to take out their name and replace it with Sunderland's instead. Ready? A guy's getting his hair cut. He says to the hairdresser that his dog never barks when Sunderland loses. 'Okay, what does the dog do when they win, then?' asks the barber. 'Don't know, man, I've only had him for a year!'"

"Ha, ha, ha! Great one, Gabby. Good for you. I like it. We must remember that for the pub, Didge," laughed Jinky.

The banter went on and on; and needless to say, the thirty minutes flew by. It was time to pay the bill and say our goodbyes. It was then massive hugs and handshakes all around, followed by an exchange of phone numbers. I did, however, just before we went our separate ways, manage to slip a few euros into Jinky's pocket without anyone noticing.

We were welcomed on board the catamaran by the captain and crew, who had prepared massive carafes of coffee, accompanied by delicious pastries. After the safety instructions, it was time for the one-hour cruise to the island. Our group consisted of fourteen paying customers: four girls from Sweden, with the rest being, like ourselves, couples from different parts of Europe. Gabby and I sat admiring the views on the captain's "bridge," an open-aired, canopy-covered space on the highest point of the boat.

We headed into the wind, the catamaran gliding smoothly and expertly over the white-tipped waves. However, it wasn't long before we were in the shelter of the bay, anchored securely just off Dia Island. First up was free time to swim, snorkel, and use the other equipment provided by the crew: a stand-up paddleboard, water carpets, and floats. Gabby and I decided to swim to one of the nearby sandy coves and walk along the small beach, our hands entwined together. On returning, we swam on our backs, side by side, holding hands briefly before having to paddle like crazy to remain afloat. For some reason, we both got an attack of the giggles, which made the swim even more haphazard!

When we arrived back on board, the captain and crew were busy preparing a delicious Mediterranean dinner of grilled fish, salad, and different local vegetables. Two large tables had been prepared, and we found ourselves on the inside table with three other couples. The conversation inevitably flowed, and the *craic* (a Gaelic word meaning "fun" or "a great time," pronounced "crack") was good. Afterward, we returned to the bridge, snuggling in together, sipping our fruit juices in total intimacy and oneness.

"I've decided to start learning German when I get home," I said to Gabby.

"Oh, that's great. You know something, Rob? They say it's best to learn in situ and to actually live in the country. I hear there's a good language school in Frankfurt!"

"Is there now?" I replied. "It would be ideal for my language learning to live with a local family, that's for sure. Don't suppose you'd happen to know anyone with a spare room I could stay with?"

"Yes, I might just happen to know the ideal place!"

"Hmm, that would be really, really nice," I said with a grin. "I bet your family are awesome."

A peaceful, restful silence followed, but not for long.

"Rob, I don't even know your last name."

"It's Wilkinson. Rob Wilkinson."

She said no more, just smiled at me, then asked another question that was obviously on her mind. "Do you like . . . kids, Rob?"

I remembered the first day we had met and all she had told me. But my answer was spontaneous and straight from the heart.

"I adore kids, Gabby, absolutely adore them. I'd love to have four, two girls and two boys, if my wife agreed and if it all worked out. What about you?"

"Same," she said, and her smile was even bigger this time. I took her hands in mine, kissing and caressing them.

"Hey, everyone, get ready for the sunset," shouted the captain. Greece's location on the Aegean and Mediterranean Seas makes it the perfect place to see some of the best sunsets in the world as the sun disappears out of sight, casting different colors and tints across the sky, clouds, and ocean. (Dave and I had experienced this previously in Zante.) This was the final piece to the perfect day—a romantic sunset on the way back to harbor, still out in the open sea.

The sky was ablaze with Gabby's favorite orange and reddish colors in the distance as, little by little, the sun began to disappear off the end of the earth. But life would go on; and without a single doubt, the sun would reappear tomorrow, bringing light, heat, life, hope, even romance. And although this was our last full day together in Crete, we knew the same applied to us—that the vacation romance had gone one step further, that our relationship was not over by a long shot, that our love would continue to grow stronger and stronger, even in separation, day after day after day.

"I love you, Gabby Weber."

"I love you, too, Rob Wilkinson."

And our senses became overpowered and overwhelmed as we kissed again, swept up by tenderness, affection, fondness, warmheartedness, and love.

CHAPTER 10
GOODBYES

I couldn't take my eyes off her. It was early morning; and she was still asleep, having dozed off in the taxi en route to the airport. Her face was cute, peaceful-looking, content. What a difference from eight days ago. Then, her eyes opened, and that lovely smile spread across her face.

"Hi, you dozed off," I whispered after gently brushing her lips with mine.

"Come closer, Rob. Snuggle in a bit longer. I'm going to really miss you."

"Same. But the time will fly by, and we'll soon be together again."

It's all in the eyes—or, at least, in Gabby's, whose I could read perfectly. In that first encounter, there was fear, hurt, sadness, immense pain, and suffering. That second night, I detected mischievousness and playfulness—a kind of naughtiness, even. Now, there was something else, something very different, her pupils dilated with . . . what?

Love is an amazing thing. Falling in love is the most sensual experience in the world. You just can't get that person out of your head, out of your thoughts and mind. It brings beautiful feelings and desires. It produces a need to spend time together, sharing, laughing, helping, supporting, encouraging, sometimes consoling. It's a connection, both inside and out. Inside, in the soul, in the heart: inner feelings of peace, of oneness, of genuineness and sincerity, of caring for the person at a deep, deep level, of wanting the best for the person and, if need be, of wishing them to smile again, to be restored to their normal self.

Outside, there's the obvious physical attraction, which is important as well. It's all about spending quality time together and being at one in each other's company. It's all about contact—with the eyes, the brush of the lips, a passionate kiss, touching through fingers and hands. It's all about emotion—showing that emotion, expressing it. It's all about communication—chatting away together, laughing and smiling, quietly whispering in the ear, listening to what they have to say, and being interested in all aspects of their life. It's all about expression—every day, telling them how important and beautiful they are, how much they mean to you, how much you love them. And when separation comes, feelings of sadness, unhappiness, and want inevitably arise.

But we had already agreed not to be sad on this our last day together in Crete. Instead, we had promised to look to the future, to meet up in Northern Ireland during the October holidays and in Germany over Christmas.

So, what were my dilated pupils, feelings, and emotions telling me, telling Gabby? That we loved each other. That we were deeply in love.

"Gorgeous, I've something to tell you."

"Hmm. What is it, Rob?"

We were still cuddled close together in the taxi, so I could easily reach over to whisper gently in her ear.

"I've told you this already, but I just want to keep on saying it every day of my life. I don't say it lightly. In fact, I've only said these words to one other person. This break in Crete has been the best time I've ever had. To have met you, Gabby, has been the best thing that's happened to me. I love you. I love you. I love you." And the tears began to flow down my face. I couldn't stop them, nor did I try.

"Come closer, my love," she murmured. "You know the pain I had to endure. You got me through it; and I have never, ever felt like this before in my life. I love you, too, Rob. You mean the world to me, and I want to be with you forever. I love you deeply as well."

We held each other in our arms, giving one another gentle kisses and caresses and whispering deeply affectionate words. Love was the answer. Love was what it was all about. Love would keep us together over the days, weeks, and months ahead. Until we met again, when everything would dilate—our pupils, our feelings, and our emotions. Roll on, October. Roll on, Christmas. Roll on, life!

PART TWO

CHAPTER 11
FRANKFURT

I came across the article quite by chance while researching things to do in Frankfurt. It was the last six words in particular that grabbed my attention, reminding me of something Gabby had said in Crete. The synopsis, which I've expanded somewhat, went something like this:

It was Max's job to accompany his little sister Anna to kindergarten every school day. The Bauers were, in many ways, the typical middle-class family: two working parents raising two children in a nice suburb of Frankfurt. Their business was successful and meant a lot to Hannah and Dieter, but it was the kids who were the jewels in their crown. They were devoted to them and loved them deeply. Their beautiful son and daughter meant the world to them.

It was a glorious September morning, the sun reflecting brightly off the calm waters of the River Main. Max and Anna were very close, chatting away nonstop on the bus into the city. This should have been followed by a short ten-minute walk to Anna's kindergarten before Max headed off for his own school. But the calmness and beauty of the day was soon to change drastically.

As they took their usual route, which involved walking down a narrow street, a car came flying down the road, hit the curb, and mowed them down. They both died instantly on the spot. The driver got out of the car to briefly check on the state of his car, never once looking at the dead bodies sprawled on the pavement. He swore loudly, got back in, revved up the vehicle, and fled off into the distance at lightning speed. It was a red Ferrari F8.

September, however, was not all gloom and doom. A very special day was looming, the start of which Gabby later divulged to me, with considerable glee and joy. The recap, which I've broadened a little, went something along these lines:

"Not long to go now, sis. You'll be back in his arms in no time!"

"Nineteen days! Oh, Stef, I really miss him. I've never, ever been like this before, so deeply in love."

Just then, Mom burst in.

"Happy birthday, my darlings," said Hilda Weber as she hugged Gabby and Stefan tightly. "I know we're meeting up with Gramps and Grandma tonight, and you'll no doubt receive something nice from them; but I wanted to give you mine now, if that's okay. Hope you don't mind, but they're both more practical gifts, rather than personal. I'll give you your cards later. Now, you go first, Stefan."

It was a small package, more like an envelope, but it contained quite a bit of money.

"Oh, Mom, that's awesome! It's perfect. I can put the money toward my next trip with my friends. Still plenty of the world to explore! Thank you, Mom. I love you." The inevitable hugs and kisses followed before Mom spoke again.

"Your turn, Missie. I hope you don't mind, but I decided to get you something more useful and functional. Hope you like it. It's up in your bedroom."

"There was nothing up there, Mom, before I came down for breakfast," responded Gabby.

"Just wait, my love. I hope you won't be disappointed," said Hilda as all three rapidly ascended the stairs.

Inside Gabby's bedroom stood a small bed and there, to the side, was a massive cardboard box propped against the wall.

"Aren't you going to open the box?" asked Stefan.

"Well, okay. Wonder what it can be. Maybe a mattress?" responded Gabby. She walked over to the side of the huge box, pulled back the side flaps, and looked inside. "There's nothing inside, Mom. It's empty. Oh, my goodness! There's someone inside at the very back. Ah! Oh, it's you, Rob! Oh, oh, oh!"

That's when she lost it, a bit like I had done at the food and wine tour in Heraklion. She literally pulled me out of the cardboard box and threw herself into my body, wrapping her arms around me, pulling me in tight, the tears again streaming down her face like a continuously flowing river. Actually, I was exactly the same. The joy of seeing her, of being in her presence, of breathing in her beautiful aroma totally overwhelmed me.

"Happy birthday, babe," I managed to get out. "I love you."

That's all I could say. We were still lost for words, each caught up in the moment, a moment we never wanted to end. Absence makes the heart grow fonder, so the old proverb goes. This was very true—our affection, our endearment, our fondness and tenderness for one another were even greater and stronger than six weeks ago. How was that possible?

And then, we kissed. Mom and Stefan were still standing thirteen feet away. Who cared? We certainly didn't. We were in our own little world again, oblivious to everything and everyone around us—engrossed, absorbed, riveted, and overflowing with love and affection.

Eventually, I managed to whisper in her ear, "Guess who organized and planned all this, Gabs? I think you should go over now and give Hilda a massive, gigantic hug!"

Gabby did just that, running across the room into Hilda's outstretched arms, the tears of joy, happiness, and delight again flowing freely. "What can I say, Mom?" she said. "The best birthday ever! You know how much I've missed him. I love you with all my heart. Thank you, Mom."

When things calmed down a little, we went downstairs for coffee and biscuits, communicating via all three languages. It was now my turn to hand out presents. They were both rather small-looking and envelope-sized, like Mom's gift to Stefan. Gabby went first. She opened the package to reveal a printed receipt I had made for a mystery tour for four people the day after tomorrow. It was no mystery to Mom—she had helped me choose somewhere suitable where the twins hadn't visited previously.

"Four, Rob?" she asked.

I just waved my hand around the table; it was to be all four of us, of course.

"You know me so well, Rob. How I love my family—and you. It's perfect."

"You're perfect, Gabby," I murmured back, giving her a gentle kiss.
"Your turn, Stefan."

It was another small package, which he immediately tore open with relish. It may have been small, but it hit the mark: a VIP tour of the Deutsche Bank Park—Eintracht Frankfurt's soccer stadium—for three people later that morning. He was ecstatic.

"Aw, man, that's awesome!" he said. "Thanks! You're definitely coming with me, Rob, and you, too, sis."

"Thanks, Stefan," I replied. "I booked it for today as Hilda said you'd be free. It would have been for four people, but she said she was busy."

"I've got dinner to prepare!" she replied. Actually, she had told me earlier something to the contrary: that she had already booked a table somewhere special to eat out.

"And after that," said Gabby as she leaned over to whisper in my ear, "it's our time!"

Mom and Stefan must have known it was something intimate and personal that was just said, but there was now such a rapport established between us all that no embarrassment or awkwardness was felt whatsoever. Stefan was easy to get along and chat with; and although he didn't speak Spanish, his English, just like Gabby's, was near perfect. In fact, Mom seemed to understand a lot more English than she let on.

What a morning! It had gone better than Hilda and I had planned. Stefan had done his part, too, as had Gabby, in a sense. Her reactions were spontaneous and natural, her personality bursting forth with such expression, charisma, charm, and, of course, love. There was such an allure to her, a kind of magnetism and appeal drawing us closer and closer together.

Hilda, as might be expected, missed nothing, the look in her eyes saying it all. She knew that her daughter was now profoundly happy and content, at peace with herself, extremely satisfied and fulfilled. And she knew where all these beautiful feelings came from, causing them to overflow in such torrents and overabundance. She knew just how much Gabby and I loved each other, how much we were in love. Now, it was her turn to whisper in my ear, after coming over to give me a kiss on the cheek. "Thank you, Rob, for everything."

What could I say to that? I really didn't need to say anything. Actions often speak louder than words, as the saying goes. Or, as someone else has expressed it, words are from the lips; actions are from the heart. I stood up, pulled Hilda in, and gave her a massive hug back. Our embrace really summed up everything: that I felt a belongingness and kinship with this family, that I felt accepted and included, that I was fully respected and loved. What a morning, indeed. But there was still a great deal to look forward to, to savor, and to enjoy!

CHAPTER 12
THE STADIUM TOUR

T ram 21 took us south from the main railway station to the aptly-named Stadion, the last stop on the line. This iconic stadium was built on the site of its famous predecessor, the celebrated Frankfurt Waldstadion. It has now been totally refurbished and is a multifunctional center, used not only for soccer and American football matches but also for concerts and other large gatherings. The oval complex, built on the edge of the city with forests and floral areas close by, looked amazing, its name emblazoned in massive letters on the roof (which lights up at nighttime).

We arrived just in time for the 11:00 a.m. English tour and were warmly welcomed by our guide, Ulrich, and shown directly into the press room. This was, of course, where the manager and players were interviewed; and since it was a VIP tour, we were allowed to take pictures of each of us in the hot seat. Ulrich then played a short video as we sipped coffee and ate cakes and pastries. The Stadion was officially opened in 2005, having a construction cost of €126 million. It has a capacity of 51,500 and, with a convertible-style retractable roof, is the ideal location for big events, especially in times of inclement weather. The video featured glimpses of matches from the 2006 World Cup held in the park, adding that some of the matches from the recent European championships also took place here as well. Next up was all the technical stuff: the complex was built using over two-and-a-half million cubic feet of concrete and twelve thousand tons of steel, etc.

We then moved on to the trophy room and found the cups, medals, and other items presented in a small glass cabinet. I was quite impressed, but someone else wasn't.

"It's not very big," said a pimply young teenager wearing a Bayern Munich hat. Who on earth comes on a soccer tour wearing colors from an opposition team? Karl, of course. You know the type.

"The trophy room in the Allianz Arena is massive," he continued.

I managed to hold my tongue—barely! I could see Stefan and some of the others were annoyed.

"Yeah, at least we were the only German side to win a trophy in Europe in 2022," replied an obviously peeved Ulrich. "That was the second time we've won the UEFA Europa League, and we've also won the DFB Cup five times. Let's move on to the director's box, everyone, for some of the best views in the house!"

As we entered the actual interior part of the ground for the first time, I could see what Ulrich meant, the open-aired section offering superb views of the pitch and stadium. From what I could see, every seat and standing area had direct views onto the turf, with no columns or pillars obstructing the view. I was immensely impressed. Guess who wasn't, though?

"It's nowhere near as big as the Allianz," Karl sniped.

"Well, you're not in Munich now, are you?" I finally snapped, annoyed at his lack of courtesy as a visitor. It was more the tone of my voice than the actual words that put him in his place—for now.

My comment produced a massive smile of gratitude on Stefan's face—and Ulrich's as well.

"It's time to descend to the changing rooms, everyone," he said. "We'll start with the away team, shall we? Follow me."

The opponent's place turned out to be neat and comfortable but, like most grounds, not overly impressive. However, that could not be said about the home team's area. It was spacious—luxurious, even—each player having their own personal locker and peg area with their respective shirt number painted on the door. There was also a large center space, obviously used to get the players together in a group to fire them up for battle. At least, that was my impression of how it should be. I'd heard some managers didn't bother with that sort of thing, not even for a local derby.

I'd also heard of others who were superb motivators, such as the manager from a small town in Scotland called Darvel, whose non-league, sixth-tier junior team humbled a side fifty-six places above them—Aberdeen, from the Scottish Premier League. It was one of the greatest upsets in the Scottish Cup's 149-year history. He talked about the average man living to an age of seventy-seven years—or, put another way, for forty million minutes—and implored his players to give their best for the next ninety minutes—only for ninety out of that massive forty million figure.

"When the whistle goes," he said, "be prepared to give everything you've got . . . We can win this; we can achieve anything we set our minds to."

They did, and they won the game one to nothing. Having played rugby for a provincial side in my earlier years, I knew how important it was to lift the team's spirit, to remove any fear of the opposition, to believe in ourselves, to motivate the timid—no matter if the opposition was from one of the bigger teams in the capital. We country boys gave our all; and if we did lose, it was not without a fight. What a contrast to some of these overpaid so-called "super stars" of today!

Anyway, as it was Ulrich's five hundredth tour, he had organized a special competition just for us, the winner receiving a mini-cup trophy. On one section of the wall hung nine pictures of different players, with a whiteboard underneath each one. The idea was to take turns going forward and writing the name of a team any one of the nine had played for. Getting it wrong or being unable to guess meant you were out. The players were Manuel Neuer, Johan Cruyff, Cristiano Ronaldo, Mario Götze, Son Heung-min, Thierry Henry, Mo Salah, Antonio Rüdiger, and Zlatan Ibrahimović. The whiteboards were soon filling up with all the obvious answers: Bayern Munich, Schalke, Barcelona, Man Utd, Real Madrid, Juventus, PSG, Ajax, Eintrach Frankfurt, Chelsea, Arsenal, Roma, Stuttgart, Sporting, Inter Milan, Liverpool, Al Nassr, LA Galaxy, etc.—with some appearing more than once. Gradually, however, only two contestants were left standing to fight it out: Karl and Stefan.

Zlatan, with all his travels, was the obvious subject, though he already had seven teams written on the board. It was Karl's turn, but he was clearly struggling. As the time passed, Ulrich eventually had to force him to concede. It was now down to Stefan. If he could remember one more team, he was the winner. He was concentrating hard, a massive frown on his forehead. Suddenly, his eyes lit up. Inter Milan was the obvious choice for Zlatan, but what about AC Milan? It was worth a shot—and he was right! Karl's face, red and angry-looking, was *not* a sight for sore eyes! Ulrich presented Stefan with the small prize, adding that there was still one more name to go on Zlatan's list: the Swedish team Malmö.

The tour was coming to an end, but we now did what every player at every soccer ground in the world does: walk through the tunnel (if there is one) onto the pitch itself. Once again, I admired the design and layout of the arena: the front row seats were only a few yards from the edge of the pitch, giving the best views possible to the spectators and helping to create the incredible, vibrant atmosphere the Deutsch Bank Park is famous for. Karl remained silent, for a change.

CHAPTER 13
ZUDKA

O n arriving back home in the mid-afternoon, we spent a few very relaxing hours chatting, having a cup of tea, and then getting ready for Hilda's big surprise—dinner in an elegant restaurant somewhere in the center of the city.

The aforementioned eatery turned out to be in a small, chic restaurant called Die Zudka in downtown Frankfurt. Despite being quite small and quaint, hidden away in almost a backstreet alley, it was extremely popular. Fortunately, Hilda, as organized as ever, had booked a table for the four of us, plus her in-laws, the Webers, and Stefan's girlfriend, Ella, who worked as a doctor in one of the main hospitals.

It was noted for being a clean, modern gem of a place, serving delicate, sublime dishes bursting with fresh, intense flavors. Someone had described it as "a culinary experience; certainly a reason for visiting Frankfurt." Well, I, of course, had other reasons for visiting Frankfurt, but this could be added to the list if it lived up to all the reviews it was receiving.

On entering, we were shown to our table, where I was introduced to Klaus and Lina Weber, who had already arrived, and also Ella, who, after a quick change, had come directly from her work. You know how you take an instant like or dislike to someone? Thankfully, in this case (unlike earlier at the Deutsch Bank Park), there was an instant bond and rapport between us all. These were kind, decent, honest, genuine, down-to-earth folks, who had no doubt worked hard over the years to provide for their family and friends. That was the Webers, though so many of those attributes could be applied to Ella, as well. She was a bubbly, fun girl, full of life and vigor and a joy to meet.

Lina noticed Gabby's beautiful bracelet she had put on for the special occasion. I had observed it earlier as well: four little groups of floral petals, with a tiny diamond encased in the middle of each arrangement. It must have been worth quite a bit of money.

"I see you're wearing the bracelet I gave you, darling. That belonged to my mom. It makes me so happy to see you using it."

"Thank you so much, Nanna. I'll treasure it forever."

Klaus, who, like so many Germans, spoke English very well, had a hearty, warm, infectious laugh. He took my hand in his and gave it a firm but not overly tight handshake. He neither gripped it like someone using a pair of pliers or gave it the limp, listless shake of someone lacking interest. It was hugs all around from the two other ladies.

I could see straight away that Klaus and Lina absolutely adored their grandchildren, giving them massive hugs, pats on the back, and kisses, along with their presents and cards. These, along with mine and Ella's, had to be opened right away. It was more cash for the twins, who, having just turned twenty-four, were delighted to top off their bank accounts once again. Then, Ella's presents had to be opened as well.

Next came the menus, the owner personally introducing himself and explaining what was on offer. We were advised to try as many different dishes as we could, as each one had its own unique taste. It sounded like good advice, so we did just that and didn't have any regrets. As the evening progressed, it seemed that each plate was tastier than the last. Our eclectic ordering produced a massive range of aromatic dishes, varying from soups to scallops and lobster, from pastrami to ravioli, from duck to rack of lamb served with honey-lemon roasted vegetables, and then a mouth-watering selection of desserts. There was quite a vegetarian and vegan selection as well.

And throughout the evening, the conversation ebbed and flowed non-stop. Klaus turned out to be another big fan of the Eagles (not the band) and roared with laughter when Stefan told him all the details about today's tour. The little trophy was proudly displayed on the table after first checking to see how up-to-date Mr. Weber was on Zlatan.

The amazing service continued as the staff brought in an extra little surprise: a chocolate log dessert covered with sparklers and candles, all aglow and sparkling brightly. Even the owner reappeared to start off a round of "Happy Birthday" in German. This had to be followed by the English version and then, so Hilda would not be left out, the Spanish as well. It was a terrific evening in every way, each item coordinated down to the smallest detail and the attention by the staff first rate. Not to mention the fabulous flavors—it was a taste experience beyond compare.

We raised our glasses of water and soft drinks to toast the birthday girl and boy. We raised our glasses to Mom for organizing such a wonderful evening. We raised our glasses to the owners and staff. And we raised our glasses to each other before Klaus rose to his feet to speak.

"Take everything in moderation, including moderation!"

After the inevitable laughter and polite applause, it was my turn for a toast from Ireland: "May your troubles be less, and your blessings be more. And nothing but happiness come through your door."[4]

Hilda and Gabby then begged me to repeat the story about my best friend Dave ("no-hair Bloomer"). Even the diners at the neighboring tables, along with the staff who had been listening in, burst into laughter at the punch line.

I whispered into Gabby's ear beside me, "Enjoy your evening?"

"Hmm," she purred. "Sure have. But the night's not over yet. Can't wait to get you in my arms later on!"

"Too right," I hummed back. "Can't wait, either!"

The inevitable handshakes, hugs, pats on the back, and kisses followed as we said our goodbyes, taking our respective taxis home. Ella had been invited to the house for dinner the next night, so we'd be meeting up again quite soon. Klaus and Lina warmly invited me to join everyone at their home on Christmas Day, which just added to the gloss of the evening. I found them to be some of the warmest, most genuine and sincere people I had ever met—just like the whole Weber family.

It had been a great day. Gabby's birthday surprise and the time spent with all the family had made it such a memorable and enjoyable fourteen hours. But now, it was our time, just Gabby and I, together, in the living room. After a lovely hug and kiss, we simply sat down and chatted non-stop, holding each other's hands, at times smiling or laughing, at other times more serious and thoughtful. And throughout it all, we looked into each other's eyes. Again, those

---

4   Dorien Kelly, *The Last Bride in Ballymuir*, (n.p.: Pocket Star Publishers, 2003), 30..

incredible eyes of hers fascinated and enchanted me, a kind of playful energy radiating from them. They were a calm and serene blue color, not dissimilar to the beautiful, tranquil waters of the Aegean Sea we had admired so much on Gramvousa Island. They seemed to lighten up and sparkle in my presence.

I was enthralled and bedazzled, especially as the pupils dilated, getting bigger and bigger. Above all else, however, it was the look that told me everything. Tonight's look matched the stare I got on that second evening spent together in Crete: a look of warmth, tenderness, love and deep affection for one another. We cuddled together in perfect harmony and oneness. How long had we been apart? You'd have thought it had been a lifetime! It was time for bed.

"This has been my best birthday ever, Rob. Thank you again so much. Sleep tight."

"You, too. Sweet dreams."

As I headed back toward the spare room, it was my turn to smile profusely. What a birthday, indeed! I hoped for plenty more like it to come!

CHAPTER 14
MYSTERY TOUR NUMBER 1

The next morning, after breakfast, we chatted about our plans for the day. Stefan and his friends were off go-carting; and Hilda had other arrangements, so it was just the two of us—perfect!

"Anything you'd particularly like to do?" Gabby asked.

"I would like to visit paradise," I replied.

"Paradise, here in Frankfurt?"

"Yes, you remember? Jinky's paradise!"

"Oh, of course, haha. The Steiner Bar! Yes, let's do that. We can even take some selfies of paradise for him to drool over on his phone! And I've got a few other parts of Frankfurt I'd like to show you, too, if you're game?"

"Sounds fabulous. I'm totally in your hands."

"Okay, but it's my treat today. I got quite a bit of birthday money yesterday. Deal?"

"Of course. Thank you," I replied.

Gabby was bubbling with excitement, full of life, full of joy. This was her "mystery tour," and she was loving it, playfully teasing throughout, her instructions and questions in German without any translation whatsoever. We received a massive smile and hugs all around from Hilda, who was so happy for us both.

We took the tram into the city's center and, after a short walk along the promenade, arrived at the Eiserner Steg in time for the one-hour cruise. It was a beautiful September morning, the River Main relatively flat, the sun's rays reflecting off the gentle ripples from the light wind. Soon we were off, heading toward the Western Harbor, captivated and enraptured by the stunning views of this dynamic city. Skyscrapers appeared to almost fight for the best location in this part of Germany's financial capital. The fiscal center certainly stood out; and with the clear blue skies in the background, it really was an imposing and impressive sight.

But Frankfurt is a city of many contrasts; and as the boat headed back toward the Eastern Harbor, we were soon admiring fabulous views of the Old Town, the museum embankment and the delightful-looking buildings and pubs.

"Do you like our beautiful city?" Gabby asked, noting my contented mood.

"The city's beautiful, and so are the people—one in particular!" I replied, leaning over to kiss those delightfully soft lips.

"I'm taking you to paradise now," she answered.

"What, massive hugs and kisses already?" I purred.

"Haha. That comes later!"

We strolled casually, hand in hand, chatting nonstop, back toward the financial district and to the Steiner Bar and Restaurant. It was time for some deliciously classic German food. On arrival, we took a quick look at the large beer garden, laden with vines, plants, and flowers, where, no doubt, Jinky and Didge had spent many an hour. After taking a few pictures, it was then back inside to the warm and cozy interior and to another shared table—the place, just like the atmosphere, was hopping!

The menu is apparently based on recipes from monastic times, the traditional favorites such as sauerkraut and Vienna schnitzel (thin, tenderized meat that is breaded and fried) with potato accompaniments proving to be the most popular. It was all in Gabby's hands; and when the food and ice-cold fruit juice arrived, we dove in, sampling them both. There was nothing monastical about the portion sizes—they were enormous, especially the two massive Frankfurters, which meant the phone had to come out again for more pictures to be sent to the Boro lads.

"Remember when we first met, Rob, and you bought that delicious baklava to share, the best in the world, you happened to say? Well, it's time to share the best apple strudel on the planet—with ice cream, of course!"

"Along with the best coffee in the world?" I teased.

"It's good. But maybe that's pushing it a bit!" she answered.

Beside us sat a rather prim and proper family: a man in his mid-sixties, a very young lady, a baby, and a three-year-old boy. Eventually, I plucked up the courage to speak to Granddad.

"Fine-looking grandson you have there, sir," I politely said.

"He's not my grandson. He's my son!" came the angry reply.

I didn't know where to look, what to feel or say. What I did feel was the table shaking to my left where Gabby sat. When I turned to look at her, her face was pointed in the opposite direction, her body shaking with laughter and hilarity. It was time for Gabby to ask for the bill and to leave; but she was in no rush and was quite happy to take her time, thus prolonging my embarrassment.

Having been fed and watered, Gabby then led me back into the heart of the Old Town, to the iconic Römerberg Square.

"Wow! What an amazing place! It's absolutely stunning," I blurted out enthusiastically.

She was delighted with my totally genuine reaction, for this was definitely a sight not to be missed. Everything was so Old World-looking, as if we were literally stepping back in time: the picturesque medieval buildings, the half-timbered houses, the Gothic church, the cobbled streets, and the massive Römer City Hall complex—the main administrative area for Frankfurt.

"Wait till you come back for Christmas, Rob. This wide-open space you now see is transformed into a winter wonderland, bursting to the seams with the Christmas markets."

"Can't wait, Gabby, just can't wait. Thanks for such a wonderful day."

"It's not over yet; follow me. We've seen the city from the river and from street level. Now, it's time for an aerial view."

We walked hand in hand, stopping to peep into some of the quaint little shops on the way. Soon, we had arrived at the Main Tower skyscraper in the Innenstadt District. The slim, fifty-six-story, 656-foot glass-structured building had two public viewing platforms, and it was not long before we were taking the elevator up to the fifty-third floor and then climbing the remaining thirty-three feet via a staircase. The views that awaited us were breathtaking, first from the enclosed viewing gallery and then, higher up, in the open-air walkway, one of Frankfurt's highest vantage points. There wasn't a cloud in the sky, so we could see not only the whole city but further afield into the distance as well. It was fun to observe the Main River meandering lazily into the beyond until it disappeared out of sight. Gabby was again buzzing, so happy at my obvious delight and happiness.

"There's one of the telescopes free now, Rob. Let's have a look."
I went first and was again mesmerized by the panoramic views.
When it was Gabby's turn, I stood behind, wrapping my arms around
her, hugging her tightly—yet another one of those never-ending
intimate moments.

"Beautiful," I murmured once again, bringing back wonderful
memories from our second day together in Crete. She giggled and
giggled, obviously remembering how our relationship had really
commenced after that one, single word!

"Thank you for a truly wonderful day. I've really enjoyed myself!"
I spoke into her ear.

"Me, too. By the way, Mom's cooking one of her favorite dishes
for us all tonight: German goulash. Hope you haven't tried it before?"

"No, I haven't. It sounds delicious. I'm very much looking forward
to it."

We were soon back at home to be warmly greeted by not only
Hilda, Stefan, and Ella but also the tantalizing aroma of the slowly
simmering goulash wafting through the house. It turned out to be as
good as it smelled—and looked. German goulash is slightly different
from other types, containing big chunks of meat with lots of sweet,
caramelized onions, spices, a strong beef broth, and tomato paste—all
of which contribute to the thick, intensely flavorsome and delicious
taste. And just like lunch time, the helpings were enormous, the stew
served with bread dumplings and roasted vegetables on the side.

They all seemed to be watching me closely as I took my first bite
and knew immediately it was an instant success. I gave a positive
nod of affirmation. An unpreventable groan of pleasure rumbled
from within! It was sumptuous: not just the thick, slightly spicy,

deliciously flavorful soupy stew but also the browned, sweet-tasting roasted vegetables and the bread dumplings, something I hadn't eaten in years. Everyone burst out laughing. Hilda's eyes were sparkling—she had wanted to cook something really special for me, and she'd nailed it.

"What incredibly delicious food, Hilda!" I blurted out in Spanish.

The conversation was in full flow. Gabby was babbling away rapidly in German, though I did hear my name being mentioned, followed by another outburst of laughter and giggling—guess it was all to do with my embarrassing moment earlier in the Steiner.

Ella had recently finished her shift and, being somewhat dehydrated, was drinking glass after glass of water. As she was on call that night and the next day, sadly, this meant she wasn't able to accompany us on the next day's second mystery tour; at this time of the year, there would have been plenty of spaces available up to the last minute. All the water she was drinking reminded me of a funny happening that occurred some time ago when I was in a work meeting, which I then shared with everyone.

"For a bit of fun, the leader requested certain items to be brought to him as soon as possible. A 'fork' was his first item; and everyone flew to the kitchen cupboards, determined to be back before anyone else. A "vacuum cleaner" came next, followed by various other items. I wasn't having any luck until he said a 'glass of water.' Again, everyone flocked to the kitchen. I, however, had other ideas and, grabbing an empty glass from the table, ducked into the nearby bathroom and scooped out half a glassful from the nearest water supply—the toilet!

"'Yes!' I exclaimed as I returned before everyone else. 'This'll impress him.'

"'Thank you,' said the boss, downing it in one gulp!

"'Oh, goodness!' I exclaimed, putting my hand to my face. Then, realizing the dire situation I was in, quickly added, 'Erm, you must have been thirsty!'

"Thankfully, the toilet had just recently been flushed!"

Everyone at the table again erupted with shrieks of laughter! What an evening! What a night! But Hilda wasn't quite finished yet. For dessert, she had purchased a stunning-looking *schwarzwälder kirschtorte* (Black Forest cake) and now placed it in the center of the table. Our mouths watered as we gazed at the generous covering of chocolate with heaps of cherries on top. Below that were three layers of chocolate sponge, each one smothered in more cherries, cherry juice, jam, fresh buttermilk cream, and a compote made from morello cherries. Delicious—and totally palatable—as we all proved again and again! Following that with some decaf coffee made the ideal end to yet another exceptional day, almost. A kiss, a cuddle, and a chat followed.

CHAPTER 15
MYSTERY TOUR NUMBER 2

S unday morning was my last full day in Frankfurt—our last whole day together, for that matter, as I was flying home the next day and Gabby had to go to work. The twins were intrigued about today's tour, especially as bathing suits were a requisite.

We all made it into the city's center to the pickup point for the early 8:00 a.m. start. However, we were soon on the warm bus, greeting our guide, bus driver, and fellow tourists as we found some vacant seats, fortunately, at the very front. Everything seemed perfect to begin with, but not for long. Condensation was forming on the windows, reducing visibility, and shortly afterward a tourist came forward requesting for the air conditioning to be turned on. This worked wonders on the visibility, but in no time another tourist appeared, complaining about the cold and asking for the air conditioning to be turned off!

Five minutes later, with the windows steaming up again, the first tourist reappeared. He was not a happy man: "I told you to put the air conditioning on. You can't see a thing out of the windows and my wife can't breathe properly. Get it turned on *now!*"

"Sir, I did turn it on until another passenger came forward to complain about the cold," replied the guide. "I'm trying to please everyone."

"Well you're not trying hard enough!" said the tourist in a raised voice, placing his hand forcefully on the guide's shoulder. "Put it back on, or I'll give you one!"

What did he mean by that? A one-star review? A punch in the face? This was getting out of hand, and maybe what I said next didn't help: "Maybe we should vote on it?"

Gabby was not amused. "Oh, Rob, don't get involved. You're only making matters worse."

She was right, of course. My sense of humor was totally misplaced, and I sheepishly apologized.

The air conditioning was back on now but at a cost for the tourist. Our guide was on the phone to the head office, reporting what had happened. Gabby informed me that if there were any further issues, another bus would be sent to remove the guilty party.

What a start! But things did get better as we made our way toward one of Germany's most charming and historic cities: Heidelberg, almost fifty miles south of Frankfurt. It is also one of the country's most visited, with over one million tourists from all over the world making the trip each year. As we approached, we could see why: the views of the old city were, frankly, majestic. From a distance, the place looked like a picture postcard—the old bridge providing pedestrian access across the river, the delightful church and brown-roofed buildings in the center, the imposing castle, surrounded by lush vegetation, perched high above. It was truly stunning.

En route to said castle, we passed by Germany's oldest university, founded in 1386. It is one of Europe's most reputable centers of learning. In fact, the whole city is buzzing with students, not only from the various universities but also from the internationally renowned scientific research institutions.

It was time for a tour of the famous castle, the most important Renaissance structure north of the Alps. We were led along the northern side of the complex through the Burgweg path into a vast, long courtyard more than thirteen hundred feet long. With a total floor area of over fourteen acres, it is one of the largest palaces in Europe. Other highlights included the extremely interesting Apotheken Pharmacy Museum, with many strange contraptions inside and one of the largest wine barrels we had ever seen; in fact, it is one of the biggest in the world.

Yet for me, the highlight of the tour was still to come: the views from the hill on which the ruins of the castle are located. I say ruins because, sadly, the thirteenth-century construction has suffered over the years, mainly due to wars, fires, and the weather—though it has been rebuilt to some extent. However, those views were to die for: the city below, the two old bridges spanning the calm waters of the river Neckar, and the verdant countryside both behind and beyond; a picturesque sight indeed!

Our guide then took us to see the old town directly from the castle by means of a cobbled path. We passed a small square, then a larger market square close to the famous Church of the Holy Spirit. It was then on to the main shopping area, a mile long in length, making it one of Europe's longest pedestrian streets. But we were only heading in one direction: first, to the eastern end to admire and walk through Karl's Gate (the name bringing a smile to our faces), and then on to the famous old bridge, constructed in the eighteenth century.

The tour party now had a while to browse around the shops, have lunch, or hike up to some of the surrounding hills and scenic areas. The four of us took our time, casually strolling back through the streets, enjoying each other's company. Eventually, we found a delightful little restaurant down one of the side streets and were soon enjoying a delicious selection of Bavarian cuisine—*schweinshaxe* (pork knuckle), *schweinebraten* (roast pork), *weisswurst* (sausages), and lots more of those fabulous dumplings, all washed down with water for Gabby, Hilda, and me, with Stefan preferring a soda.

It was great to get to know Hilda even better. She joked in Spanish about her time in Madrid and its notorious summers, the hot, dry, scorching heat almost unbearable in places.

"There's a lovely phrase the Madrileños use: *¡Bonito invierno, verano infierno!* Lovely winter, summer inferno! Have you heard it, Rob?" She giggled.

"Yeah, I hear they all escape to the coast during July and August, leaving only the crazy tourists behind!" I smirked. "One of whom was me, of course! Actually, to alleviate my thirst, I had a delicious glass of ice-cold *horchata*. It is a tasty, refreshing, and nutritious natural drink made with tiger nuts, milk, water, and sugar. Healthy for the heart, reduces cholesterol, and full of vitamins—perfect! Mind you, I had a job finding Miguel and José's kiosk, one of the few still in business. Did you ever get to try it?"

"Too right! Once, when Franz visited me, we . . . " She stopped short, the smile disappearing from her face in the blink of an eye. Then came the tears. The twins weren't fully aware of what had happened, but they had obviously heard their dad's name mentioned and had a fair idea of what was going on.

The next thing I did was a purely natural reaction. I stood up and opened my arms to her. It was exactly what she needed. Who else could she come to, to open her heart to, to let out her emotions? Not her in-laws, who were still grieving themselves, and certainly not her children—she had to be strong for them. Just like Gabby in Crete when she was hurting, Hilda reacted in the same way, jumping up from her seat and throwing herself into those open arms, the tears flowing incessantly, her body shaking, her sobbing intense. I looked at Gabby, who nodded her head in approval. I began to gently pat Hilda's back, whispering words of encouragement.

"I wish . . . I wish you could have met him, Rob," she said. "The two of you would have got on so well together. He's . . . he's the spitting image of Klaus—handsome, of course, great sense of humor, soccer-crazy, adores his family and his children. And . . . and me, of course."

"I wish I could have, too, Hilda. When my wife, Julie, passed away from cancer, I knew she was safe in God's hands. I found immense comfort in talking to her as if she was, in a sense, still here with me, watching over me, wanting the best for me. I miss her immensely, just like you must miss Franz."

"I do indeed; I feel a bit embarrassed."

"No, no, Hilda, definitely not. We've all been there—in a similar situation—at one time or another. It's not easy."

She was beginning to recover and gain control once again, as she knew she had to. The words we had both said seemed to bring comfort and healing. The tears certainly did, releasing endorphins and feel-good chemicals, bringing relief to the soul, heart, and body. How good is that? What's embarrassing about that, especially for us men? Surely, something that helps us to express and release our pent-up grief, emotions, and deepest feelings can only be a good thing. Something that soothes the brain, bringing relief from stress, that helps us cope with our painful sentiments, bearing comfort, healing, and even strength—what's wrong with that? Absolutely nothing, in my opinion. I picked up a clean napkin from the table to dry my face.

It was soon time to return to the bus for the next part of the tour. I took Gabby's hand and gave it a tight squeeze. She then took Hilda's, who, in turn, took Stefan's. We felt like a unit, each one supporting the other, looking out for their interests.

It was a good feeling, which only got better when Gabby playfully whispered in my ear, "I truly love you, Robert Wilkinson!"

"I love you, too, Gabriella Weber, really deeply."

And so on to the next part of the tour: into the Black Forest, close to the border with France, some forty-nine miles southwest of Heidelberg. Baden-Baden is one of Europe's most beautiful health resorts and best-preserved spas, with an international reputation for top-notch healthcare. The hot springs have been in existence for over two thousand years, their popularity resulting in a UNESCO World Heritage Site listing in 2021.

The official tour included a visit to the immaculately maintained gardens and parks around the Kurhaus Spa Resort, its famous casino noted for the overindulgence in decor and incredible design. Indeed, the whole place emanated a sense or feeling of wealth and affluence, with grand palaces, noble avenues, and luxurious villas all in abundance. With the incredible backdrop of lush vegetation, bushy trees, distant mountain ranges, and a bright and cloudless blue sky, I began to feel I was in another world.

The unofficial tour (mine) involved a visit to one of those aforementioned spas, the famous Divina Spa. The massive complex, covering more than ten thousand square feet, is set in beautiful natural surroundings. We had only one-and-a-half hours for our visit, and time was tight; so we were really thankful that there were no lines to hold us back.

As this was my treat—and Gabby's actual birthday present—I obtained an entry pass in the form of a wristband, enabling us to purchase drinks and snacks from the café and bar inside. After renting towels and robes, we quickly changed; and dumping our bags into lockers, we entered into a water haven, consisting of hot and cold pools, spa waterfalls, hot springs, hot tubs, water slides, loungers, saunas, whirlpools, relaxation areas, and heated lounges. We were soon unwinding in another realm, in total relaxation and comfort, running around like excited children exploring all the different areas.

The inner pool was massive, the enormous windows providing fabulous views of the beautiful gardens and patios outside. We couldn't wait to jump into the water; it was like entering a steaming hot bath. Soon, we were splashing each other, trying to dunk the other person underwater, even Hilda getting involved. One of the reviews I had read stated that the complex was "more like a theme park, a time for relaxation and the healing of mind, body and soul!" All of these concepts seemed to apply to Hilda, who, after surprising me from behind and thus managing to give me a good dunking, burst out laughing. The twins were stunned. It was the first time they had heard those sounds so prolonged and seen such joy in their mom's face in over three years. The healing was, at last, beginning.

Next up was Stefan's challenge at the ice pool, both of us having to jump in at the same time. It didn't look tempting or alluring in the slightest.

"Ready, Rob?" he asked. "Let's see who's the bravest. After three, then. One, two . . . three!"

I dove into the freezing water and felt my breath immediately taken away. How on earth do those incredibly brave women go swimming in Kilkeel Harbour in the frosty Irish Sea on Boxing Day, raising money for charity (as do many people in other parts of Britain and Ireland, and beyond)? No doubt, coming directly from the piping-hot spa bath made it even worse.

Although my face didn't quite turn blue, it mustn't have been far off, hence the lion's roar that came from within—and the hoots of laughter from all the Webers. For yes, Stefan had somehow managed to step out at the very last second. However, Gabby was having none of it—when she spotted an opportunity, she pushed him from behind; and in he went, roaring like an elephant! Hilda was in stitches. We all were!

The outer pools brought back memories of my visit to the thermal baths close to Machu Picchu in Peru. These were certainly more luxurious, containing a unique mini-tunnel allowing direct access from the inside, with superb lighting effects from every angle under the water. The perfect background was provided by the indoor pool, where the lights also shone brightly through the massive windows. It was such an amazing sensation to be outdoors in the cold mountain air yet feeling so warm and tranquil in the hot spa water—almost like taking a hot bath in the Antarctic.

Time was passing, so it was then either a quick dash in the open air or a swim through the mini-tunnel again for a visit to one of the heated relaxation areas. We then lay back on sun loungers while waiting for the food and drinks to arrive, chatting nonstop.

"I see there's a lovely cake stand in the café, Rob," said Gabby. "Don't be tempted to eat the whole lot like last time!"

"Haha! I'll never live that one down!"

"What's that, sis?" asked Stefan.

"Did Mom not tell you, Stef, about Rob's battle with the cake stand in Crete?"

"Erm, I think time's about up, guys. We should maybe start to head out?" I said, trying to change the subject.

We made it back to the bus just in time to hear the guide announce an addition to the trip: a short visit further into the Black Forest to the glorious Mummelsee, a fifty-six-foot-deep glacial lake left behind by the last Ice Age.

When the announcement was made, Hilda let out an exclamation. "Oh, that's where Franz and I used to come for a weekend's camping and . . . "

Then, the silence followed once again. We were very worried after what had happened earlier in Heidelberg.

"And, you know, for a romantic weekend!" she continued.

It was laughter this time, instead of tears, with comments like "Naughty Mom!" thrown in.

As soon as we arrived, Hilda completely took us by surprise: "Quick, everyone, we've only fifteen minutes. Follow me!"

She led us rapidly down one of the main paths toward the lake, then suddenly veered off down a little-used track. Eventually, the vegetation and forest came to an end as we stepped out onto a perfectly even, grassy patch with incredible views of the flat, calm basin and the mountains in the background.

"This was our little secret camping spot. Pretty impressive, eh?" uttered Hilda in German (and then in Spanish for me). She was like Gabby in so many ways.

I went over to her, pulled her in for a hug, and said, "You're pretty impressive!"

Gabby, as usual, missed nothing and, after grabbing Stefan, came and joined in the embrace, all four of us forming that unbreakable unit again, and so enjoying each other's company. Then, it was back to the bus for the relaxing journey home.

Later that night, we talked about Gabby's upcoming visit to Ireland during the October holidays in just over two weeks' time. How could we be sad at tomorrow's parting? Two weeks was nothing to have to wait.

Then, she whispered romantic words in my ear. "I know I've told you so many times already that I love you, Rob," she said, "but after today, I love you even more, if that's possible. It wasn't what you did for me, although that was out of this world; it was what you did for Mom that means everything to me. You made her laugh again, helping to restore her to her normal self. You made her whole. Thank you, thank you, thank you."

I left her room feeling elated and contented.

PART THREE

CHAPTER 16
ACROSS THE MILES

Needless to say, Gabby and I were in regular contact over those two weeks, sharing our stories and plans for her trip to Ireland. On the whole, these were happy conversations from a distance; and I looked forward to her calls immensely. However, there was one exception to this, one piece of information that was not at all pleasant. I could tell from the outset that the news was not good, as Gabby immediately burst into tears. Eventually, when she had calmed down somewhat, she told me what had happened.

"Rob, remember we talked in Crete about how Dad had been killed four years ago as he was walking across a pedestrian crossing? Well, it's happened again to two young, innocent children walking happily to school. The driver was totally smashed, drunk, and inebriated. He was driving a red Ferrari F8. Does that ring a bell, Rob?"

"Menzel! Oh no, Gabby, surely not?"

"Yep. Less than three months after being released on parole, he's struck again."

"I remember reading about the incident involving the Bauers online, Gabs. That's sickening. Shocking."

"And so unfair, Rob. If fairness and justice had been meted out in the first place, he would not have been paroled after three years and

117

those two beautiful children would still be alive today. I mean, that's three people who have died because of him—three. He was way, way over the minimum alcohol limit, speeding in the downtown, and failing to stop, in my Dad's case, at a pedestrian crossing. How could that be an accident, and how on earth could the judge be so lenient as to not impose the maximum sentence in the first place? You tell me."

"I'm afraid I can't, Gabby, and I'm totally in agreement with you. The system seems to be heavily stacked against the victims."

"It doesn't get any easier as time goes by. I still miss Dad terribly, every single day. Anyway, that's not all, Rob. It gets worse. Mom visited the Bauers. They live in the same neighborhood as Ella, who was able to pass on their address. It wasn't easy to get inside, though. She knocked on the door for a considerable amount of time before Mr. Bauer's patience snapped. He told her to clear off, or he would call the police. It was only when Mom slipped a newspaper cutting through the letter box about Menzel's previous conviction that the door finally opened and he let Mom in."

"Hilda's amazing," I replied.

"She knew only too well the agony the Bauers were going through, Rob. I think that sometimes, in such a situation, it can be helpful to talk to someone who has been through a similar experience."

"A bit like us in Crete, Gabby? Helping each other to overcome our griefs and sufferings?"

"Good point, Rob. Yes, it's a lot like that. But, Rob, she was not prepared for what she saw inside: the room in total disarray; the deep sadness in their faces; their sunken, dark eyes; their cheeks thin and hollow from a lack of sleep and food; their overall gaunt, haggard, almost skeletal appearance. She remembered her own misery, pain, and agony, not to mention the loneliness and depression and how difficult it had been to survive, to keep on going, to not cave in and give up. Only Stefan and I have kept her alive, with the need to provide for us, to help and support us. But the poor Bauers now have nobody. Their two treasures have been torn away from them, removed from their lives forever.

"Mom said she broke down. In fact, all three, I believe, were in the same state: shedding tears, sobbing and weeping uncontrollably, their bodies shaking and swaying. Eventually, their crying turned to quieter whimpers and then, silence, before sitting down to talk things through, each one sharing memories and recollections and even photos of their loved ones from happier days."

"Oh, Gabby, that's tragic. Just totally tragic. It's heartbreaking."

"At least it ended well, Rob. Mom suggested putting out all the details on social media, press, and news channels to stir up support and to fight for justice. She felt that Menzel could not get away with it again. That people needed to know about the suffering the victims go through. She asked if they'd like to be involved as well, not expecting an answer, instead just leaving our contact details. But she soon knew they were on board—she said she noticed a change, that instead of despair and hopelessness, there was now something else: a determination, a resolve, a desire to go on—a fighting spirit, even. *It's all in the eyes*, was the phrase Mom used, knowing full well they were now committed to the cause.

"Just before she left, she gave them a massive hug, instructing them to stay healthy and strong. She said she felt a togetherness and oneness with them, a bond that hadn't existed before, a sense of solidarity and communion."

"Ah, Gabby, at least, as you said, it did end on a positive note. I want to hear any updates when you get to Ireland. Hilda's amazing. And so are you."

We changed the subject and chatted for a few more minutes before hanging up. Eight days to go and counting. The time would fly by; and in no time at all, we would be able to communicate directly to each other, instead of across the miles. I couldn't wait.

CHAPTER 17
ARMAGH

It was good to be back at Belfast International Airport once again. It was even better to be there to collect the love of my life. I checked the arrivals board.

"Yes!" I exclaimed to myself. The Lufthansa City Line direct flight from Frankfurt had arrived right on time!

It seemed to take forever; but it was probably only about forty-five minutes before she appeared, dropped her case and bags, and ran straight into my open arms. As so often happened with us, all the emotions seemed to explode at once—joy, shouts and peals of laughter, hugs producing feelings of happiness, excitement, affection, and love. It felt so good to be in her arms again, to cuddle in and smell her gorgeous aroma.

"*Ich liebe dich*," I said.

"I love you, too. Haha. Well done, Rob. Good for you!"

"I've started my German lessons—just a beginning, mind you. I know we've only been separated for a little over two weeks, but I've really missed you, Gabby."

"Me, too, Rob; Mom as well! And, of course, Stefan and Ella, Klaus and Lina and Karl and—"

"Haha, don't think he's missed me one bit! Come on. Mom and Dad can't wait to meet you, not to mention Dave, Jacqui, and the kids."

It seemed like no time before we were pulling up outside the elegant Georgian building located directly opposite the beautiful, tree-lined mall in Armagh. Mom and Dad were waiting and watching from the window. The large, white door swung open; and Gabby was soon receiving a fabulous, typically Irish welcome: hugs, kisses, more hugs, and non-stop banter and questions.

Eventually, she managed to get a word in: "So pleased to meet you, sir, madam."

"Oh, Gabby, it's just Martin and Isabel," replied Dad.

"Come through to the kitchen, love, for a nice cup of tea. You must be exhausted after your journey." Mom took her by the arm and led her down the long, narrow hall.

"Wow! What a beautiful garden," Gabby exclaimed. "And the flowers are still in bloom, even at this time of the year. How do you do it?"

"I talk to them every day and give them plenty of TLC," joked Mom. "Actually, we've had a fabulous summer; and autumn has been quite mild, which has been the main reason. You've certainly timed it well. It's a good forecast for your stay."

The next thirty minutes reminded me of the time spent in the little tavern in Agia Roumeli, when we sat down for a lovely lunch with the Italian couple, having just completed the Samaria Gorge trek. I was mesmerized then, looking into that ravishing face, listening to her interacting with such eagerness and enthusiasm. And I was captivated now as she responded to all the questions fired at her from every direction. I could tell she was an instant hit; Mom and Dad really, really liked her.

Eventually, I was able to show her upstairs to the guest room, giving her time to unpack and freshen up. Then, it was back down for dinner: stuffed pork fillet with all the trimmings—delicious Glens of Antrim Maris Piper potatoes, veggies, gravy, and apple sauce. This was the favorite dish of my sister Karen who, along with her fiancé, Nathan, joined us for the evening meal. The main course was followed by one of my favorite desserts—homemade lemon meringue pie, fresh out of the oven, served with ice cream.

It was then Dad's turn to prepare his own version of Irish coffee for us all, the thickset cream sitting perfectly undisturbed on top of the delicious hot coffee, non-alcoholic liquor, vanilla extract, and light brown sugar below. These were downed in the front lounge, where a blazing log fire awaited.

What an exquisite day! I could tell Gabby already felt at home, totally at ease and at one with the whole family. She took this opportunity to hand out presents she had brought, which where all gratefully received. Karen was a teacher as well, so they both had plenty to talk about, comparing the educational systems in both countries. However, time was passing. It had been a long day for Gabby, and it was now time for bed.

It was Sunday morning, and we were all off to worship. Mom and Dad attended the nearby parish church called Saint Mark's, set on top of a hill, with stunning views of the mall below and the cathedral in the distance. Gabby and I traveled a little further afield to my local church, and she was amazed at not only the attendance—it was bustling inside— but also the open-plan layout, with comfy individual seating and large projection screens.

"Wow, this is awesome, Rob! I've never been in one like this before."

We were seated beside another good friend of mine, Greg, along with his girlfriend, Rose. Greg and I went back a long way, having played soccer for one of the junior teams. Perhaps it was due to his height or, more likely, his natural ability and talent that he was still playing while I wasn't. He was doing rather well, actually, playing in goal for Portadown, one of the top teams in the area. Suddenly, the band struck up, playing one of my favorite songs.

"This one's called 'Way Maker,' Gabs, originally written and sung by an amazing Nigerian singer called Sinach," I said. "Jesus is our Way Maker, shining His light and showing us a way out of the darkness. Awesome, eh?"

However, it was the sermon that really touched her; by the end of the service, she was uncharacteristically quiet, obviously contemplating and absorbing all that had been said. Rose picked this up immediately, taking her hand, chatting intensely, and even praying with her. Then, I proudly introduced her to all and sundry on the way out. Actually, they knew all about her already; the whole church had been praying for us both.

Sunday dinner was always on me, and today was no exception. Mom and Dad spoiled me rotten during the week—I rarely ever ate on my own. So, while Karen and Nathan took Gabby out for a drive and walk, I got stuck with the cooking. It was stuffed roast chicken, but with a twist. First up, the marinade: finely chopped fresh basil, oregano, crushed garlic, seasoning, lemon juice, olive oil, and a touch of water. This all went "inside" the bird, between the skin and breasts, which enhanced the flavor incredibly. Accompanying the chicken were some veggies, roast potatoes, Yorkshire puddings, sausages, and gravy. It was absolutely delicious, if I may say so!

Gabby certainly did. "Wow, Rob. You're a man of many surprises. Think I've hit the jackpot with you!"

There she was again, expressing herself so openly, without a care in the world. I just loved her for it and could see, from the twinkle in Mom's eyes, that she felt exactly the same.

"I want you and Rob to accompany me first thing tomorrow morning, Gabby," Mom said. "I want to treat you to a few bits and pieces from our shop."

My granddad had opened a store in the town some time ago. Dad eventually took over the running of the shop and, together with Mom, enlarged and modernized it. Mom would make sure Gabby was well-pampered tomorrow.

For dessert, it was a bought rhubarb crumble with custard or ice cream, followed by coffee and a relaxing evening by the fire.

Armagh is the ecclesiastical capital of Ireland and home to two astoundingly beautiful cathedrals, both named after the famous Saint Patrick. Legend has it that he built a stone building on a hill back in AD 445, on which one of the massive cathedrals now stands. In 1994, Armagh was granted city status and is known as "the city of saints and scholars." Gabby loved it, not just for my family and the warm welcome she was receiving, or for the mall with its stunning Georgian architecture, or for the enchantment of the municipality but also for the friendliness of all the people we met on the way up to the shop.

"It's as if everyone knows me, Isabel. They're all so friendly!" she said. "Yet I've never met them before in my life!"

"Ah, my dear, that's Irish hospitality for you. We're some of the warmest, kindest, friendliest people in the world. You know, where I grew up in Milford, we used to leave the door unlocked all day long, and nothing was ever taken or stolen. Apparently, we are now living in better times, in a more civilized world. I'm not so sure of that."

"Haha. I can see where Rob gets his wit from!"

"I love your bracelet, by the way."

"Thank you. It belonged to my great-grandma. It means a lot to me."

Mom smiled broadly, taking Gabby's arm, pretending she needed it for support. But the truth was, Mom was a great judge of character; and she was very, very impressed with this girl: with her gentleness and goodness, her genuineness and tenderness, her thoughtfulness and kind-heartedness. She knew how I, her son, had suffered over the past two years from heartbreak, despair, and the traumatic and harrowing time everyone had gone through. But she also knew, without a single doubt, that Gabby was the reason behind the dramatic change that had occurred. I was now more like myself: smiling, joking, full of life once again.

"I like you, Gabby," Mom finally said in her ear, loud enough for me to hear. "I like you a lot. Welcome to our family!"

On our return, Gabby's face lit up with that incredible smile of hers. Mom had gone over the top a little, buying her new underwear, a sweater, and other clothes of the latest design—made in Germany, of all places! But that was not all, by any means. I could see that a deep rapport was developing among all the family. We sat down to a simple lunch of homemade lentil soup with sides of cheese, salad, fresh wheaten bread and, just for me, a fruit soda loaf. All was washed down with piping hot tea; even the cups were warmed up in boiling water beforehand!

In the afternoon, we went for a walk around the mall, popping in to visit one of the neighbors, who insisted we have shortbread and tea with her. This was followed by another massive family meal together, with two desserts on offer this time. Welcome to Ireland, Gabby!

Indeed, it was time to explore more of this amazing island. I had taken a week's vacation from the property investment office; so the very next day, we were heading off to beautiful Donegal.

CHAPTER 18
DONEGAL

We set off the next morning after breakfast, taking our time to admire the incredible scenery of Lough Erne, an amazingly attractive lake system with more than 150 islands. The sun shone brightly, and there wasn't a breath of wind—Mom had been right about the weather.

The two-hour journey flew by; and in no time, we had arrived at the luxurious Lough View Lodge, superbly located in the Blue Stack Mountains looking down on Lough Eske, with the Atlantic Ocean in the distance providing the idyllic backdrop. I had managed to book a very good offer of two night's bed and breakfast, plus one evening meal in two of the deluxe single suites.

The first phase of the brand-new Scandinavian-styled complex was now complete. Later down the line, individual log cabins with their own outdoor hot tubs would be constructed, dotted around different scenic locations. But for now, the main area functioned as a hotel with rooms, bars, and reception and dining facilities.

A turf fire burned brightly next to the reception desk as we checked in. Gabby was immensely impressed, taking in the stunning décor, which included impressive Nordic-style interiors, under-floor heating, wood burners, and high-quality paintings, tapestries, and pictures on display in every nook and cranny.

But it was the room, or rather suite, that impressed her the most. It was a good size, having its own hall, TV, a medium-sized bed, and a little table with comfy chairs by the window, with breathtaking views to look at. The designers had got it spot on—it was all about those views. The huge sliding glass doors opened out onto a lowered wooden deck, with glass frames all the way around the balcony, hence maximizing the field of vision. And what a sight—not only the Lough below and the sea in the distance but also the trees and bushes on either side helping to create a oneness and harmony with nature.

The same standard applied to the inside. They had thought of everything: bathrobes and slippers, complimentary toiletries, bottles of water, fruit, and freshly made cakes. But it got even better when Gabby walked into her spacious bathroom. It was equipped with all the modern conveniences, including a walk-in power shower and a large bathtub. There was even calming bird-sound music playing gently in the background.

"Can't wait to try that out!" exclaimed Gabby delightedly, looking at the bathtub. "Oh, Rob, never mind the Steiner Bar; this really is paradise!"

"I know, love. Let's grab a quick bite out on your veranda. Mom kindly made us a packed lunch."

And quick it had to be, for we were booked for the 2:30 p.m. departure slot for the "Orienteering—Expect the Unexpected—Challenge." Soon, we were back at the reception area, dressed in trainers, running gear, and a lightweight, windproof jacket; for although the weather was once again kind to us, it would inevitably be quite chilly in the mountains.

"Hi there," said the pretty receptionist, looking straight into my eyes. "I see you're from Armagh."

"Yes, I am," I replied, somewhat coldly. "This is my girlfriend, Gabby, from Frankfurt. We're here for the Lough View Challenge."

"Yes, of course," replied the receptionist, a little put out and now much more formal. "The runners depart at fifteen-minute intervals; so at exactly 2:30, I will hand you a map of the area and a second sheet with the coordinate points you will need to locate the ten control markers. You *must* do them in numerical order, please. When you arrive at each point, look out for a lilac-colored triangular board and copy whatever is on it. Then, move on to the next one as fast as you can. We have ten groups taking part today; the three with the best times win a prize. Report back to reception with your completed sheets. Good luck, and off you go!"

Gabby immediately took control of the sheets, marking down the first location before disappearing out the door at full speed. She was in it to win it, and she rapidly started the ascent up the mountain path toward Croaghnageer East Top—though, thankfully, not all the way up! We eventually stopped, panting heavily, looking for the three-sided marker. I spotted it about twenty-two yards further up a steep incline.

"There it is, Gabby! I'll go get the letters if you could maybe plot the next one on the map?" It was good teamwork, saving precious minutes that might make all the difference.

Thankfully, the second marker involved a traverse to the west along a level pathway. Even though we were both jogging and panting, it was impossible not to admire nature's beauty at its best—Brown's Hill off to the right, Croaghnageer East Top and Croaghnageer Mountain more or less directly behind, the Lough and sea to our left, and, straight ahead, a group of three mini-loughs in the near distance.

"Over there, Rob. Beside the rock," shouted Gabby excitedly.

The second board was cleverly placed in a group of lilac heather, making it harder to spot. Then, it was down to Lough Amincheen—and the first "twist" of the afternoon. A staff member was waiting with a life vest and canoe at the ready, for the next marker was on an island.

"You go, Rob. I'll get all the other points plotted while you're away."

Fine by me. I'd done quite a bit of canoeing in the scouts, and it wasn't long before I was back on dry land to a very nice surprise: a bottle of water and chocolate bar for each of us. This hotel was just getting better and better!

It was a ten-minute jog to the next control point, located halfway between Lough Amincheen and Lough Ankeeran. Again, the views were stunning, the sun's rays reflecting off the dark water of these fabulous mountain lakes. Checkpoints five and six were easily located at Lough Ankeeran and Lough Aderry. However, it took much longer to find the next marker, for it was hidden away further into a forested area.

Then came twist number two: expect the unexpected—a zip line! Another staff member was on hand, providing safety helmets and the appropriate harness for those brave enough to have a go. The alternative was the steep path off to the right, leading down to the shores of Lough Eske. I looked at Gabby, who immediately nodded in agreement. It was a no-brainer: mount up for the zip line death slide!

Within minutes, we were descending at a fast pace, holding on to the handle tightly, whooping and shouting out in sheer euphoric joy and delight. The views must have been stunning—but my eyes were fixed only on that handle!

Yet another staff member helped us out of the harness at the bottom but instructed us to keep the helmets on: the final twist was a bike ride nearly all the way around Lough Eske. We stopped briefly at the last three checkpoints before passing through the little hamlet of Townagorm, and then came the final ascent to the reception area in the hotel.

"Oh, well done, you two," said the receptionist. "That's a fast time!"

Neither of us said a word. We were panting heavily, fighting for breath. But we'd done it and felt quite pleased with ourselves, especially as we took a seat outside in the sunshine, sipping another complimentary bottle of water and munching on a delicious homemade cookie.

"You're different, Rob," said Gabby between bites.

"And by that, you mean . . . ?"

She took her time in replying. "You're loyal. You're faithful. You're kind. You're caring. I feel I can trust you 100 percent. No, that's not strong enough. I *know* I can trust you 100 percent. God's doing a good work in you. You're *so* different from Ernst."

"What brought that on?" I asked, somewhat bewildered. It was time for the Weber pause again.

"Sorry, it was maybe something I should have told you earlier, Rob. I wasn't sure if it was the right thing to do. Actually, I wanted to tell you in person, face to face, and not from a distance. Do you remember me mentioning Ernst?"

"Yes, of course, in Crete. How he dumped you and moved on to someone else."

"Well, he came back," replied Gabby, in a low, unsure voice. "I couldn't believe it when I opened the door. What a shock! My mind was in turmoil. What was he doing here? What did he want? He apologized for not calling in advance. He asked if we could go for a short walk. No, that's not quite right. He pleaded with me to go.

"Rob, if you could have seen his face. It was forlorn, desolate, and expressionless. Was it right to go? Maybe I should just have closed the door in his face. But there was something in his eyes that made up my mind. He looked so sad and dejected, hurt and defeated, down and out, desperate even. I probably chose the wrong option, Rob, but I decided to quickly grab a cardigan and join him outside.

"Nothing was said initially as we walked toward the nearby park. It was Ernst who broke the silence, apologizing, admitting he'd made a huge mistake and that he'd hurt me. He asked me to forgive him. He said he had messed up, big time, only realizing later on how good we'd been together ('a great team' was the phrase he used), and lots of other stuff like that. He looked the part, Rob; his eyes were moist, appearing to be in such pain and agony.

"Anyway, we finally reached the center area of the park where a little kiosk sold ice cream and other goodies, attended by a pretty girl. *Let me get you your favorite, Gabs. Have a seat. I'll only be a sec*, he said. But the seconds turned in to minutes, unsettling me. I decided to quietly approach the kiosk to find out the reason for the delay. There he was, chatting away happily to the girl. I even saw him pass her his business card. Eventually, he must have turned around with an ice cream in each hand, looking for me. But I was nowhere to be seen. I had run away.

"Oh, Rob, I'm heartbroken. I should have told him to go away right at the start," she said, the tears starting to flow. "He deceived me again! I feel so stupid. And that I've let you down."

I can't deny I was somewhat taken aback and surprised. On the other hand, my feelings went out to Gabby. She could have simply covered it up, saying nothing, and I'd have been none the wiser. Instead, she had wanted to open up and share everything with me. Surely, this was what a true relationship involved, where we could share everything with each other, even our regrets and mistakes.

It was my turn to surprise her, with a smile that was worth a thousand words! She jumped into my open arms, sobbing uncontrollably, the tears flowing non-stop. I just gently patted her back, hugging her tightly, at the same time whispering assuring words of love and affection.

"Thank you for sharing that with me, Gabs. Others might not have done so. It confirms to me the type of person you truly are. Let me repeat your words back to you. You, Gabby, are loyal. You're faithful. You're kind. I feel I can trust you 100 percent. No, that's not strong enough. I *know* I can trust you 100 percent. And I believe God is working in you, too. And that excites me! As do you! I love you devotedly, veraciously, beyond question!"

We hugged, kissed, and chatted a while longer before returning to our respective rooms to freshen up. In due course, we sat opposite each other in Gabby's room in the comfy chairs by the window, taking the opportunity to call both sets of families before setting out for a gentle walk around the hotel's beautiful gardens, hand in hand, chatting amicably. It was then time for dinner in the award-winning Michelin-star restaurant, with more impressive views to admire and enjoy. The sommelier soon approached to take our food and drink orders. We chose a sort of mix and match from the four-course menu, deliberately selecting two different dishes but sharing both. Hence, it was scallops and lobster for starters, followed by a refreshing sorbet, then filet mignon in a mushroom-and-wine sauce with game chips and Mauritian fish curry, a delicious selection of desserts and decaf coffee, with more of those scrumptious homemade cookies to round it all off.

What a day! It got even better when the results were announced. We had come second in the challenge and won a delightful-looking picnic basket. Gabby had known about this activity, but the next day's was a total surprise. She couldn't wait.

The surprise came after breakfast and the thirty-minute drive to the seaside coastal resort of Bundoran, the most southerly town in Donegal. We were going horseback riding, and she was delighted. I'd pre-booked the one-and-a-half-hour beach-and-sand-dune ride, stating that we were semi-experienced riders. This was true in my case, having enjoyed galloping along one of the beaches on the Isle of Arran in Scotland. However, Gabby had never seen a horse up close, never mind having been on one.

The owner, Briege O'Hanlon, was a robust, hardworking, friendly soul who enjoyed a good laugh. We joked and bantered as I signed the disclaimer form, filling in all my personal details as well. It was then over to her young assistant, Nuala, who took charge of things and fitted us with helmets and riding boots. She told us that, as she was the eldest of eight children and was thus expected to contribute and help out, she worked seven days a week during the peak season. But she adored horses and loved her work immensely. She led us into the sand-covered arena to meet our well-mannered beauties, Felix and Champion, and to have a thirty-minute time of instruction covering the basics: mounting and dismounting, stopping and starting, and turning to the right or left. Gabby was mesmerized with Champion, talking to him and patting his soft, furry mane as they got accustomed to each other. She did have a little stumble as she mounted for the first time. After that, however, there was no holding her back.

It was another glorious autumnal day, perfect for such an outing. Nuala's horse led the way down from the equestrian center through the outskirts of the town to Tullan Strand, a vast open beach with enormous sand dunes and breathtaking views of Donegal's coastline. In fact, this shore forms part of the Wild Atlantic Way, one of the longest coastal routes in the world. There was sand everywhere, the horses enjoying themselves as much as we were. Nuala and Gabby chatted away amicably as we progressed further down the sandy parts of the near-empty beach. Yet it got even better as we finally moved on to the harder, firmer sand close to the water's edge in preparation for a gallop down the beach. This is horseback riding at its best, the rhythm smooth and graceful as the rider's body almost molds itself into the horse's back, the two becoming one.

When the horses finally came to a halt, I glanced over to see an ecstatic Gabby, hugging and patting Champion with obvious glee and joy. She loved it even more when we cantered into the surf, the horses splashing in the cool, clear water of the Atlantic Ocean.

The ninety minutes flew by before we returned jubilantly to the center. After saying our goodbyes and tipping Nuala generously, we made our way to the Sheilin Restaurant, a typically rustic Irish eatery highly recommended by Briege. We were soon enjoying delicious smoked salmon served with a salad, wedges of lemon with dill aioli dips, and—a real treat—Guinness brown bread! The rich flavor of the bread was to die for, all washed down with that inevitable cup of piping-hot tea.

It was when we got back to Gabby's room that tragedy struck: she realized her bracelet was missing. She was heartbroken, immediately bursting into tears, sobbing loudly. The wristlet was expensive—that was for certain—but it was more the sentimental value of it that was irreplaceable.

"It was so stupid of me, Rob, wearing it horseback riding," she said. "I should have left it in the car. I'm devastated."

"Gabby, it was my fault as much as yours," I replied. "You had no way of knowing what was planned for the morning; it was a total surprise. If I'd forewarned you, it would have been left in the safe in the room. I'm so sorry, my darling."

What a disaster; for, although Gabby tried her hardest to make little of it, I could read her like an open book. She was gutted.

"Listen, love," I said. "We're leaving tomorrow morning after breakfast. It's just a slight detour back to Bundoran. We can walk along the sand and have a good look."

She nodded her head affirmatively but with little enthusiasm. We both knew it would be a waste of time, like trying to find a needle in a haystack.

Dinner was a rather subdued affair in the Bar and Terrace dining area of the hotel. We should have been admiring the stunning, affluent décor of our surroundings as well as those fabulous views and the usual warm, first-rate Donegal hospitality; but sadly, we weren't in the mood and, after the meal, headed up to our rooms for an early night. However, I felt there was still something else that not only could be done but should be done.

"Gabby, I know you have your doubts about divine intervention and God's presence in this world, and I understand that fully. There's not an easy answer why sometimes He intervenes and on others not. But I want to relate a true story Pastor Tim shared with us one Sunday which I think will be helpful. He talked about an occasion when he had to cry out to God for help in a time of need. Due to his commitment to the church, he wasn't able to accompany his Peruvian wife Juana and their young son on a family visit. Unfortunately, Daniel became sick and was diagnosed as having bird flu which, at the time, was lethal. They took x-rays and blood samples, gave him strong antibiotics, and put him in a private room, all to no avail. His condition was deteriorating; the tablets weren't working. And with the bird flu pandemic worsening, flying back to the UK was not an option.

"The future was grim. Juana's voice, when she called, was naturally full of fear and hysteria. What could Tim do in such a situation? What could he do so far from his loved ones? He was helpless. And for a parent, there is nothing worse than not being able to come to the assistance of your child or family. The only thing he could do was cry out to God. He poured his heart out to both God and the church, praying and fasting and sharing words from Scripture, such as from Hebrews 5:7: 'During the days of Jesus' life on earth, he offered up prayers and petitions with fervent cries and tears to the one who could save him from death, and he was heard because of his reverent submission.' The pastor sensed that God was present and listening.

So, he handed the situation over to Him, immediately experiencing, for the first time in days, incredible peace of mind.

"Meanwhile, Juana went to the KLM office in Lima to see if the hospital was right about Daniel not being allowed to fly. They confirmed this was the case but suggested getting a second opinion, recommending the doctor used by the KLM staff in Lima. They also pointed out that, due to the peak season, all the planes flying from Lima to Amsterdam were fully booked.

"Two things happened. First, the doctor turned out to be a total blessing: 'What are these x-rays for? I don't need them. And all those tablets? Throw them away; they are totally useless. The boy doesn't have bird flu—he has pneumonia. All he needs is penicillin. He can return immediately to the UK on the next available plane!'

"Wow! What an answer to prayer. But what about the next problem, trying to find space on a plane bound for Amsterdam, then on to Belfast? Juana went back to the KLM office to find there had just been a cancellation: two seats were available at the very back of the plane! Would she like to have them? 'Hallelujah! Praise the Lord!' she shouted."

"Oh, Rob, that's marvelous!" Gabby said. "Truly amazing!"

"I know, awesome, eh? When the folks appeared at the arrivals building, Daniel didn't go running into Tim's arms with a massive smile on his face, as was the custom. Instead, he sat in his buggy, as white as a ghost, with no smile whatsoever. But they were home. Daniel was safe. Their own doctor confirmed the diagnosis as pneumonia, and it wasn't long before the big fella was back on his feet and Tim was praying, 'Thank You for Your mercy, Lord, for Your goodness to us in our time of need. Thank You for hearing our cries and for Your compassion, grace, and love.' So, my darling, I think we, too, should pray and cry out to God in our moment of need. Would you kneel down beside me at the bed while I pray?"

"Of course, Rob. Please do pray."

"Dear Father God, we come to You in our moment of need and desperation. We know You love us, that You are here present with us, listening to our cries for mercy. Dear Lord, You know what this bracelet means to Gabby, the value attached to it that can never be replaced. And so, we ask You to help now, to somehow enable us to get it back. Please, Father. In Jesus's most precious, holy, and wonderful name. Amen."

"Amen," echoed Gabby. "Oh, Rob, that is so comforting to be able to do what we have just done. I feel incredible peace in my heart!"

"Christianity is all about a personal relationship with the living God, Gabby. We can talk to Him, cry out to Him, share our joy with Him. It's got me to where I am today. I couldn't have made it without Him and the support and love of family and friends. It's been good to pray together. Shall we make it a habit, every evening, just before going to bed?"

"Yes, I would like that very much. Good night, my love."

"Good night, darling. Sleep tight."

The next morning, Gabby was almost back to her normal self. It was a huge blow, but what could be done? Life had to go on. As we munched our toast, chatting away, my phone rang.

"Hello," I answered, not recognizing the number. "Yes, speaking. What? Oh my goodness! Just a minute, Briege, while I put the speaker on. Yes, we can both hear you now. Please repeat what you just said."

"I was wondering if Mrs. Wilkinson has lost a bracelet? Nuala found one in the arena this morning."

"Yes, yes!" shouted Gabby at the top of her voice, attracting everyone's attention. She had to briefly describe the wristlet in detail, confirming that it was indeed hers. Then, she jumped into my arms to celebrate, tears of joy flowing anew. Everyone was staring at us, but who cared—we certainly didn't! What an answer to our prayers!

We couldn't wait to get back to the room to kneel down and praise the Lord. Then, it was back to the reception desk to check out and collect one packed lunch (we had the picnic basket as well) ordered from the day before.

We were soon reunited with Briege and Nuala, Gabby giving the girl a massive, whopping hug, continually thanking her from the bottom of her heart. I gave her a wad of euros, not bothering to count how much it was. I couldn't care less. I was just so thankful to Nuala, Briege, the whole world, and God! It meant that much to me. But so much more to Gabby! She explained all about the bracelet, that it had belonged to her great-grandmother, who had passed it on to her daughter, who had given it to Gabby. Briege was so happy for us; and indeed, we could have stayed on chatting for ages, had we not a long journey ahead. It was time to move on to our next destination.

On the road north, we conversed about all that had happened. Gabby was amazed at Nuala's honesty—the bracelet was very valuable. She was also amazed at God's answer to our prayers and asked if we could return to the church on Sunday. But I could tell she was mulling over something else, something that had stuck in her mind from that morning.

"Briege called me Mrs. Wilkinson, Rob. What do you make of that?"

"We must look like the perfect couple, my love," I replied happily.

"We are the perfect couple!" she answered. The look in her eyes and that big smile said it all.

It was a two-and-a-half-hour drive to the Romaris Causeway Hotel near Ballintoy in Northern Ireland. However, before that, there were a couple of unmissable stops en route, the first one at Malin Head, the northernmost point of mainland Ireland, located in the townland of Ardmalin on the Inishowen peninsula.

It was time to get some fresh air and enjoy a walk along the cliff top. This area was one of the film locations for *Star Wars: The Last Jedi*, providing a remote and barren setting. We could soon appreciate just why it had been chosen—the coastal scenery was dramatic and rugged, while, at the same time, having a charm of its own with an abundance of birdlife, beautiful beaches, enormous sand dunes, and dramatic landscapes. We presently came across one of these at a place called Hell's Hole, a subterranean chasm which burst into life when the incoming sea flowed into the cavern, crashing ferociously against the rocks.

In a short time, however, we were on our way again and presently spotted a delightful place to stop. There was a lovely grassy area just perfect for sitting down to eat and to admire the stupendous views of the nearby loughs and sea. The weather was once again kind to us as we enjoyed the delicious packed lunch and picnic basket from the hotel, chatting away about all that had happened. Gabby was still over the moon that the bracelet had been found and was continuing the conversation as we moved on to one of the most appealing lighthouses in the world. Fanad Head Lighthouse, towering seventy-two feet high, looked down on this area of outstanding natural beauty.

"Come on, Rob. The views from the top must be amazing! Beat you to it!"

The race was on, both of us eager to be first to climb those seventy-six steps to the uppermost point. We giggled and joked as we ascended at pace, Gabby gleefully pulling at my jacket to hold me back. In the end, it was a close finish as we both collapsed onto the observation rail, a little out of breath, yet still managing to let out hoots of laughter. It was only then that we realized that a guided tour was in progress, and a small, balding man with a large beer belly (or possibly a Guinness belly), who was obviously the guide, glanced at us with a look of total disdain.

"So sorry," I managed to get out between breaths. "Do carry on."

"Thank you for your permission. I will do just that," he replied, the heavy sarcasm obvious to all. "As I was saying, before being so rudely interrupted: following a shipwreck of the *HMS Saldanha* in 1811 in the waters of Lough Swilly, one of Ireland's three glacial fjords, it became apparent that a lighthouse would have to be built to prevent further tragedy and loss of life. The building you now see was designed by the greatest engineer of his time, George Halpin, and was first lit on Saint Patrick's Day, the seventeenth of March, 1817. Today, if you're lucky, you might just see some whales, porpoises, or even dolphins basking in our beautiful ocean . . ."

To give the man credit, he certainly knew his stuff and was probably doing this for free, volunteering to show tourists all the ins and outs of this amazing, and still functioning, lighthouse. We listened to what he was saying, while, at the same time, admiring the views. They impressed from every angle and direction—the Atlantic

Ocean to the front, Lough Swilly to one side, and Mulroy Bay to another, thus completing the picture.

"What a truly stunning country Ireland is, Rob," said Gabby contentedly as we held each other's hand.

"Well, it is when the weather's like this," I replied. "Sadly, that's not always the case."

We still had a fair bit to travel, so it was time to move on, heading up north once again.

CHAPTER 19
THE CAUSEWAY COAST

Along the way, I managed to fit in a brief detour to show Gabby my old school. I told her a true story about my time there when I attended as a boarder.

"One of the advantages of this was that I could commit entirely to the educational and sporting facilities on offer. (I thoroughly enjoyed playing both rugby and cricket.) One of the disadvantages was the austere rules applied after lights out in the dormitories. Conversation of any kind was strictly forbidden after 10:30 p.m. We were just young boys at the time, so it was natural to whisper to my friend to see if he'd heard the soccer results or something similar.

"Suddenly, a voice rang out: 'Talkers, out. To my study—now!'

"Discipline in those days was somewhat different from what it is now—three on the behind using a tennis shoe! So, we arrived at the teacher's office expecting just that. However, on this occasion, he simply told us to return to his office after school the next day.

"'Yahoo!' we whooped at each other on the way back to the dormitory. But that exuberance soon disappeared as reality sank in: the punishment had merely been postponed. Come 3:30 p.m. the following day, we would be back in his office!

"That night, I couldn't get to sleep. What lay ahead was constantly on my mind, the punishment awaiting. At breakfast, I wasn't hungry. During the classes, I couldn't focus properly. Finally, after what seemed like an eternity, the hour arrived for us to go and receive the discipline. We left the office somewhat relieved, if not with rather sore bums!"

"Oh, Rob, that's terrible," Gabby said. "What a horrible thing to have to go through. Where is that brute? He deserves a good slapping of his own! Tell me a nice story instead."

"Okay. As a youngster, I loved all kinds of sports, including water skiing. Every weekend in the summer, we would be out skiing on two skis, one ski, trick skis, jump skis, a disc, a chair on top of a disc—anything went! So, it was no surprise when I ended up one summer in the United States at BUNA Camp as a water ski instructor. We taught kids as young as five years old how to ski. The technique was quite simple. An instructor would ski alongside the girl or boy and, with one hand, literally lift them out of the water, their skis dangling all over the place.

"Eventually, when the skis were pointed in the right direction, the instructor lowered the child gently onto the water with a firm hand on their shoulder. 'Don't you dare let go of me!' was a common-enough cry. But we already had, and the young boy or girl was skiing by themselves.

"Then, the inevitable happened. They began to doubt, to wonder, and to disbelieve. They would turn their heads, look across at the instructor, find no hand on their shoulder, and fall into the water! Every time!"

"Aw, that's better. I liked that one," she replied. "What about you, Rob? Have you ever gone through times when you felt all alone, like there was no hand on your shoulder to support you?"

"Yeah, of course, many times. Going to boarding school at the age of twelve was really tough. I can remember saying my goodbyes to Mom and Dad after they'd dropped me off. I felt like a snowflake lost in the ocean, unsure of the future, uncertain of what lay ahead, tiny, insignificant, scared, and vulnerable. I wouldn't be seeing them again for three weeks when I could use up one of the weekend passes we were allocated. I can remember it clearly even now—it was a lovely, sunny day.

"But I certainly didn't feel any warmth—only a coldness inside, coupled with fear and nervousness at stepping out into the unknown, into a new school, a new environment, a new challenge. Even so, I quickly learned to stand up on my own two feet, to survive, to overcome, and to succeed. Made lots of good friends, did well at sport, not bad at the studies, have some very good memories. It all worked out in the end.

"You know what else I've learned through life? The need to have a figurehead to provide support, protection, stability, and strength. I know it's a little bit abstract, but I sort of realized this later in my twenties when playing for the local second's rugby team. An Irish international who played for our club was recovering from an injury, gradually working his way back into the first team, hence his appearance for our team. I cannot describe the difference his presence made to the morale of our side. To have an Irish international taking the warmup, playing alongside us, offering words of wisdom, advice, and encouragement. It was just awesome! Any fear of the opposition dissipated. An international rugby player was on our side.

"And what about the opposition? As soon as they realized who they were up against, their faces dropped! Fear set in. They were petrified. Needless to say, we won the match easily that day! Anyway, what I mean to say is, I've always had someone like that to help me—Dad, a very kind senior prefect at school, good friends in the church, and, of course, God. Gabby, that's been my experience, my testimony. No matter what problem I've experienced in life, I've always had the assurance, the absolute certainty, that I have never had to solve it on my own, that the problems and difficulties would be overcome with God's helping hand.

"I've been pondering over what you said previously about where God was when Franz died and why He didn't prevent it from happening. It's the big one, isn't it? Why does God allow suffering, loss and tragedy to happen? I've come up with two answers, for what they're worth.

"First, I think that people who go through suffering and pain change, sometimes for the better and sometimes for the worse. That's certainly been my experience, and I think, in my case, it's been for the better. Yes, before I lost Julie, I was a Christian. I went to church, prayed, tithed, etc. But in some ways, I was quite shallow, insincere, and not really deeply interested and concerned in other people. That changed when Julie passed. Her loss eventually helped me to become a more sensitive, caring, deeper person. I seemed to be able to detect or discern in certain people that same hurt, sadness, and brokenness that I had experienced. And I seemed more prepared and able to offer comfort, compassion, and assistance. I hope that's what you felt when we first met in the restaurant after Preveli Beach in Crete. I felt drawn to you, Gabby, like a magnet. I could feel your suffering, torment, and pain; and it just about broke my heart. So maybe suffering and loss helps us to have more compassion and sensitivity for others, especially to those going through a similar experience.

"Second, I think these things happen because God gave us free will, the freedom to make our own choices. One of the byproducts of this is, sadly, sin. We live in a fallen world where sin prevails, a world whose 'authority and splendor,' as Scripture tells us, have been given to the devil[5] and that is under his control.[6] So maybe we're blaming the wrong person?"

"Hm, that's interesting. And helpful," replied Gabby. "In response to your earlier comments, I can relate to those feelings of loneliness and vulnerability. I tend to doubt and fear, maybe more than I should. I agree with you, Rob, we all need someone to encourage and support us. For me, that was Dad. He was always so reassuring; he seemed to almost be able to sense when I was down, when I needed help and support. Now that he's gone, I've drawn even closer to Mom. Maybe I should grow closer to God again as well. But you know something? In the last three months, I seem to have found another sort of a rock to stand on."

"And that sort of a rock would be?" I asked.

"You."

If I hadn't been driving, I would have pulled her to me and, at the very least, kissed her passionately. All I could do was quickly glance into those beautiful eyes, returning her smile in kind and giving her hand a quick squeeze.

"Same, Gabs. You only have to ask Mom why she likes you so much. She has seen the change that has come over me since the summer; and now that Mom's met you, she knows the reason why. The answer is in these words—Gabby Weber, the love of my life."

"Oh, I love you, too, my darling."

---

5   Luke 4:5-7
6   1 John 5:19

Not long after, we pulled into the Romaris Causeway Hotel, Ballintoy, in the late afternoon. It was my first time there as well, having booked it on Dave and Jacqui's recommendations; they had been there six times already! As we retrieved our luggage from the trunk of the car, we could see why—the views were outstanding, the hotel not only looking down on the delightful village and fishing harbor but also on Rathlin Island in the distance.

The old turf fire was burning here as well. The additional extras, however, were the hot wipes offered for our faces and hands, along with a delightfully refreshing glass of homemade lemonade accompanied by Irish shortbread. We were off to a good start! Our rooms were numbers 320 and 322, but I deliberately set our bags down outside the room opposite and knocked on the door.

"Rob, you're at the wrong room," Gabby said. "Ours are . . . Oh my goodness, Isabel! Martin! What are you doing here? What a surprise! What a delight!"

Her reaction, as usual, was so spontaneous and so gratifying to observe. She was elated, almost jumping for joy, and actually did leap into Mom's arms, giving her a mammoth hug, then turning to hug Dad.

"You knew they were here all along," she said as she finally broke away, pointing her finger at me. "You arranged all this, you rascal. You're so, so . . . adorable! I love you!" She then gave me a massive hug and passionate kiss, not at all embarrassed that Mom and Dad were watching.

I just relished this about her—she was so open and expressive, nothing hidden, full of feeling and emotion, passionate and evocative, full of energy, full of life. She then sat herself down on one of the chairs and started chatting nonstop with my parents, bringing them up to date on everything that had happened, leaving nothing out. I managed to bring our luggage into the respective rooms, making a start at unpacking a few of the essentials, then returning to a room full of laughter and merriment. Mom and Dad had insisted on coming here, so I couldn't really claim the credit for that. But it had definitely been the right call—we all blended together so well, just like one happy family. We were in for a great night.

Dave and Jacqui had gone on and on about the mouth-watering food served in the hotel, and we were soon making sounds in total agreement. The vegetables and other ingredients were locally sourced when possible, and, of course, the seafood only had to travel up the hill from the Ballintoy harbor below. The furniture, lighting, and overall décor had been carefully planned to create a charming, relaxing ambiance. Even the restaurant's location and choice of windows had been arranged to perfection, capturing the stunning views of the Atlantic Ocean at its best: Rathlin Island ablaze with sunshine in the near distance; and further afield, Scotland's Isle of Islay and the Kintyre Peninsula were clearly visible on a good day.

In no time at all, we were admiring those views, enjoying the fabulous food, and chatting away nonstop, Mom and Dad bringing us up to date about the shop, the garden, and the next day's *ceilidh*, a traditional Scottish and Irish (mainly) social gathering that was being organized by my brother Tom, to be held in the Bloomer's massive outbuilding in Lisburn. Then, it was Gabby's turn to display that lovely bracelet before telling the story of how it had almost been lost, then miraculously found. As for me, I was enjoying every second, seeing how, once again, she fit in so perfectly and naturally into our family. Those feelings of comfort and contentedness, which I had experienced previously on the return bus journey from Gramvousa Island in Crete, were growing stronger and deeper.

After breakfast the next day, all four of us drove through the pretty village of Ballintoy, passing the charming white church on the hill. I told them a story about my previous visit to that lovely and quaint place of worship with Dave and Jacqui.

"Dave has a fabulous, deep bass voice and, if prompted, quite often sings a solo or two. Well, in this church, you go forward to the front for communion, which we did. However, Dave was somehow delayed on our return and ended up sitting in my seat. Lo and behold, at the end of the service, the lady in front turned around to congratulate me on my fabulous singing voice! Dave immediately burst into laughter—he knew I couldn't sing a note!"

In the meantime, we descended a spectacular, steep, winding road to the little fishing harbor. This area is famed for its sea stacks and small rocky pools which lead on to one of Europe's best cliff top and wild beach walks. The producers of *Game of Thrones* were obviously impressed, as it was chosen for one of their filming locations. Yet we weren't here for those stunning walks; instead, we hoped to take a boat trip over to Rathlin Island, only to find we'd missed it by two minutes.

"Hold on, guys," said Fiona, the kind lady in the ticket office. "I'll see if I can get Gerard on the radio. Gerard, I've four more passengers for you . . . Well, I know you've left already—just come straight back and pick them up, you hear!"

"Wow, that was cool," said Gabby, obviously impressed.

"Yeah, well, he is my husband," replied Fiona. "Knows better than to get on the wrong side of me!"

On boarding, we apologized to the other passengers; but they all took it well—Gerard included. Gabby was amazed that he'd come back for us and made a point of thanking him two or three times. In no time, we arrived at the ferry port on the island and disembarked for a quick walk around the quaint little harbor. We were greeted by the sound of birds, birds, and more birds! In fact, tens of thousands of seabirds, including puffins, razorbills, and kittiwakes make that place their home. Couple that with colonies of seals, many seen lounging on the rocks, and you have a bird-and-marine-watcher's haven.

We were soon at sea once again, this time doing a circuit of the L-shaped island, admiring three more lighthouses.

Gerard gave us a running commentary. "That's the East Lighthouse we're just passing. It's the oldest of the three; and if you look below it, you will notice Robert the Bruce's cave. King Robert of Scotland was exiled here in the fourteenth century and, while in the cave, noticed how an extremely determined spider kept on repairing its broken web. Well, he thought he could do the same and was thus inspired to return to claim his throne. So, guys, we Irish are very superstitious—never kill a spider; it brings you bad luck!"

There were plenty more stories and legends from where that came from, and as we headed back to see the sea stacks and stunning cliffs, we said a prayer of thanks to Fiona for making it all possible. She might have appreciated that, but she certainly was grateful for the very generous tip she received from Dad.

We arrived back at the harbor on schedule for a delicious lunch in the quaint little café close to the jetty. It was another glorious day, so we sat outside eating homemade soup with wheaten bread, followed by apple pie and ice cream.

"How does this compare to the strudel, gorgeous?" I asked.

"Oh, it's so yummy, and the ice cream is to die for. Look at that bird over there, Rob!" she exclaimed.

I bought it, hook, line, and sinker. By the time I turned back around, a scoop of my ice cream had somehow made it on to Gabby's plate! Mom and Dad doubled over laughing.

"Don't worry, I'll make it up to you tonight," she whispered in my ear. "Lots of hugs and kisses!"

It was time to show Gabby some more sights the Causeway Coastline is renowned for; and as it was so close, our next stop was at the Carrick a Rede rope bridge. We took our time walking from the parking lot to the attraction, a journey normally of around twenty minutes but now, due to the steep path and steps, a little longer than that. The bridge stood before us, swaying gently in the breeze. We were soon traversing the sixty-five-foot span of wood and rope, looking down at the relatively calm sea below. The crossing links the mainland to the tiny island of Carrickarede and was originally used by salmon fishermen as early as 1755. Indeed, a small pathway led down to a disused boat before descending further to a rocky access point at sea level. I remembered a presentation someone at work had given, all about the need for persistence and tenacity. They had used a video of a salmon in a river as an illustration, which I now put to good use.

"These fish always come back to their river of birth to spawn and reproduce," I started out. "So, there must be a connecting tributary close by, which is why the fishermen choose this location, the rocks proving to be an obstacle for the migrating salmon. The brave fish have not only human predators to contend with but also strong currents at the mouth of the river and, further inland, rocks and other hurdles to overcome. What an example for us all of the need to persist and never give up!"

"Too right," said Gabby, taking Mom's arm. "We tasted some delicious smoked salmon yesterday, accompanied by Guinness brown bread. So good and tasty, Isabel—have you tried the bread before?"

"Oh, I sure have, Gabby," replied Mom. "That's one of my favorites, although you can't beat a good, fresh wheaten, in my opinion."

The chat continued as we headed to the highest point on the rock before turning back for the parking lot.

Our final stop that day was at Northern Ireland's most popular tourist attraction—the Giant's Causeway. We had been advised to pull in at a little parking lot about a ten-minute walk from the attraction. We took our time casually strolling down the road before taking the short bus ride to the UNESCO World Heritage site. And what a truly spectacular scene awaited us!

There were thousands upon thousands of mostly hexagonal-shaped, interlocking basalt columns, the tops of which appeared to be stepping stones. They were the result of an ancient volcanic fissure eruption, the lava rapidly cooling to form these incredible, staircase-shaped rocks. What a breathtaking view! October was a good time to visit without too many other tourists around, so we climbed up to get some fabulous pictures of the rock formations with the dark blue sea in the background.

"Can't wait to send my photos over to Mom and Stefan," said Gabby. "I've never seen anything like this. You'd think we were almost on another planet!"

"Do you know why it's called the Giant's Causeway?" asked Dad. "Legend has it that an Irish giant called Fionn Mac Cumhaill built a path of stepping stones all the way across to Scotland in order to fight his great rival, Benandonner. However, the canny Scot was having none of it, so he ripped up the track, leaving what we see today."

"We once played rugby against a team with a giant of a guy whose nickname was Tiny," I continued on the same theme. "Nobody could tackle him; he was built like a tank. The one exception to this was the smallest player on our team, who ignored Tiny's upper muscular bulk, instead concentrating on tackling low, around the legs. Downed him every time; awesome guy! Come on, Gabby, there's a cliff top trail over there. Bet the views up there are pretty good. Let's go have a look."

Mom and Dad returned to wait by the bus stop while we climbed to the top, where we were indeed justly rewarded with another immaculate vista of the Causeway and beyond. We made our way back to the folks, walking hand in hand, before taking the bus up the hill, then casually walking to the parking lot.

It was yet another relaxing, enjoyable evening for us all before having an early night. Mom and Dad would be heading back to Armagh after breakfast the next day. As the hotel wasn't overly busy at this time of the year, Gabby and I would check out of the rooms at midday after spending the morning relaxing in the spa, pool, and hot tubs. We would then go directly to Dave and Jacqui's for the barbecue and *ceilidh,* a traditional night of music and dance extremely popular in Scotland and Ireland. Before all that, though, I was looking forward to my reward for the ice cream Gabby had pinched earlier on!

CHAPTER 20
BBQ & *CEILIDH*

"This is pure bliss," Gabby groaned as we were ensconced in a whirlpool bathtub with two other guests. It was massive, capable of holding up to six people at a time. And even better, it was located outdoor in the open air, meaning we could lie back in total luxury, enjoying those fabulous sea views.

"I could lie here forever," she continued. "But maybe it's time for a swim?"

"Good idea," I replied. "Ready?"

It was a small but superbly designed pool with plants and mini palm trees in one corner, soft music playing in the background. I produced a small, padded ball to throw, each one trying to catch it like a goalkeeper at full stretch, reminding me of Greg. Next, we stood as far apart as possible, again throwing the ball, trying to make a clean catch forty times in a row without it dropping into the water. Then fifty, and then . . . oops, it slipped out of my hand!

At that point, Gabby went for her spa-pampering experience while I went outside to the hot tub again before returning to the heated relaxation area to "chill" out. They did advertise the complex as the ideal place to de-stress and get away from it all. *Too right, I* thought to myself, sipping a complimentary herbal tea, contentedly waiting for Gabby to return.

It wasn't long before we had checked out and were heading for Lisburn. Of course, there was an inevitable stop to be made, this time at yet another stunning tourist attraction—the Dark Hedges. This amazing avenue of beech trees has, over the years, almost become entwined, forming a long, mystic, wizardly-type tunnel. It is one of the most photographed natural phenomena in Ireland, and we were soon doing just that: taking pictures from every possible angle and from both ends of the lane. More photos to send over to Frankfurt!

But we had a date to keep: a special afternoon and evening in Lisburn, Gabby at last getting the chance to meet my best friends, Dave, Jacqui, and their three young girls. And what a welcome—massive hugs and kisses all round, gifts from Gabby for them all, and a large spread prepared for afternoon tea, including a wide variety of sandwiches, cakes, buns, boiled fruit cake, homemade scones with fresh jam and cream, and a mountain of desserts prepared for the evening. All this was accompanied by freshly ground South American coffee, Dave literally grinding the beans as we spoke.

Gabby was the center of attention, struggling to get a bite in edgewise as question after question was fired at her. The youngest of the Bloomer girls took an instant liking to her and ended up sitting on her knee. (I immediately got my phone out for a photo, adding it to the growing collection.)

Then, in the middle of everything, my brother Tom burst in, having just arrived from Scotland. He was in charge of the *ceilidh,* bringing not only all the gear and equipment necessary but also his two oldest boys to help. The decibel level was increasing even more as the room resounded with noise and conversation, Gabby being yet again introduced to the new arrivals. But there was still work to be done for that evening, all of us chipping in with the food preparation, tables and chairs, the barbecue, etc.

In no time, the guests were arriving: Mom and Dad, Karen and Nathan from Armagh, and other good friends from all over the Province. It had been a no-brainer to accept Dave and Jacqui's offer to host the event. Their garden was Dave's pride and joy—large and well-kept, the kitchen ideal for prepping; and best of all, there was a huge outbuilding in which to gather, chat, drink, eat, and dance.

People everywhere in Ireland like a night of music and dance, and a *ceilidh* is just perfect for getting everyone up on the floor to have fun. The word originates from Gaelic, meaning "gathering" or "party," and is a traditional, mainly Scottish folk music dance set, popular at weddings and other get-togethers. *Ceilidhs* are all-inclusive—almost nobody is left out; everyone can be involved and have a good time. And with the right instructions, each dance is relatively easy to pick up, even if you do have to watch another group closely to copy exactly what they're doing.

The first dance was one of Scotland's favorites—the Dashing White Sergeant. Tom was calling everyone up to form groups of six dancers who joined hands, forming a circle. We then turned one way for the count of eight, then the other, before breaking our circle into two groups of three. Next, the person in the middle of the mini-group had to perform various steps, feet-stamping and hand-clapping with each of the other two members, before all three got together again to form an archway, eventually meeting up with another group of three to start all over again. Or something like that! It wasn't all perfect, by any means; but by the time the music stopped, everyone had more or less perfected the dance.

It was so enjoyable. Gabby loved it and couldn't wait for the next one to start—another extremely popular dance called the Gay Gordons, named after a famous army regiment from North East Scotland, the Gordon Highlanders. This time, it was just the two of us, one of many couples who got together in one big circle. I joined my hands over her shoulder, walked forward four spaces, pivoted around, then back four steps, repeated this with Gabby pivoting around and, finally, polka-danced around the room in whatever space was available before joining up in the big circle to start all over.

When the reel finished, everyone collapsed. It was time for a rest, and it came in the form of Tom's announcement that the food was ready. We all headed out to the covered patio, where Dave and Jacqui were already serving prawn kebabs, steak, burgers, marinated chicken, vegan options, salad, rice, hummus dips, crisps, chips, bread, rolls . . . It was all a little surreal for us both as we floated from one group to the next, making a point to mingle and mix with all the guests.

But this night wasn't all about dancing, eating, and conversing. Dave took over, rattling off a few well-known ditties on his tin whistle while everyone sang along, interlocking arms and swaying from side to side. A few comic sketches had also been prepared, the best of which was performed by Greg and my nephew Jonny, along with Mom and Gabby, who had been roped in at the last minute.

It went like this: the setting was a doctor's clinic, and there was Greg on his own, waiting to be called. In came Gabby, who sat down and began coughing. Soon, Greg started to cough while Gabby improved dramatically, so much so that she departed, leaving the poor fella spluttering profusely! Next in was Jonny, who sat down. He seemed to have some sort of nervous reaction; for he immediately started jerking his leg up and down, pausing, then jerking once again. You can guess what happened next. Greg, along with his sporadic coughing, started to have the same nervous jolting action, while Jonny made a remarkable recovery and then exited. Last in was Mom, and the place went wild—she was pregnant, with a pillow stuffed under her shirt! The laughing continued as Mom took her seat.

Greg wisely waited for the racket to die down before he stood up, pointed at Mom's belly, then pointed and looked down at his own stomach before shouting out, with a look of pure horror on his face, "No way. I'm out of here!" And off he went at full pace, running out of the waiting room! The place erupted in total uproar.

This was followed by the *ceilidh* once again, then another break for coffee and desserts, and, finally, some slower music to round off the perfect evening. I was a bit like Gabby with Gerard on the Rathlin Island boat trip, thanking everyone profusely for such a wonderful time.

Indeed, all the last eight days had definitely given Gabby a flavor and taste of Ireland, and I could tell she had enjoyed every moment of it. Tomorrow was her last full day before flying back to Germany to start work; and while we would miss each other intensely, Christmas was just around the corner.

CHAPTER 21
LAST FEW DAYS

"Hands up, everyone who likes dolphins!"

Gabby let out a loud gasp of amazement, bringing her hand up to her mouth. She immediately raised her hand, as did everyone around us. We were back in church, as Gabby had requested. Pastor Tim was just starting his sermon.

"I think that's just about everyone. And I take it you'd all like to see them up close, actually touching them in their natural environment? Yeah, guessed so. I can remember a time of great joy when visiting a place called Monkey Mia in Australia. It is located in Shark Bay, Western Australia, about nine hour's drive from Perth.

"More than two thousand dolphins and twenty-eight shark species inhabit the bay; so, as you might expect, it is famous for its wild dolphin experience and is renowned for being one of the best places in the world for dolphin interaction. They say it's perfectly safe to swim and enjoy the turquoise water. Not so sure about that, but it's definitely *the* place to see dolphins up close in their natural habitat. Today, this attraction draws over one hundred thousand people to the beach every year.

"Thankfully, it was relatively unknown when I visited. I was able to touch and feed them in relative peace and quiet. One hour later, however, in the stifling heat and humidity of the outback, our old Holden panel van got a flat tire. The feeling of peace and tranquillity from the visit to Monkey Mia was soon forgotten! Today, I want to talk about a place where our joy, our happiness, and our pleasure will last forever, never ending. And it is?"

"Heaven," said Greg beside me.

"Correct. For the Christian, there is nothing more uplifting, more encouraging, more reassuring than the guarantee of eternal life. We are always planning for the future: working hard, paying off the mortgage, opening up savings accounts, contributing to a work pension, even preparing a will. It's a normal thing to do, making us feel secure, giving us peace of mind. With all these preparations, we feel we've done our best to provide for ourselves and our family for the future.

"But the Bible talks about an inheritance that is so much better than any amount of money or property we may have on earth. It talks about a home that will never crumble or be taken away. It talks about a life in the future that is guaranteed to last forever, an inheritance that is promised to every child of God—eternal life, the great Christian promise, the great Christian hope.

"We met up with some Peruvian friends recently while vacationing in Scotland. They asked if it would be possible to visit the National Wallace Monument, close to Stirling. The brochure states that this is 'a place where history is something you can touch and feel, as you trace the story of Sir William Wallace, patriot, martyr, and Guardian of Scotland.' The main attraction is definitely the high tower, with 246 steps to the top! There is only one narrow stairwell, making it quite awkward when other people are descending. But it is so worth battling on to get to the upper part, with the fabulous views of Ben Lomond and the Trossachs to the west, the Pentland Hills to the east, not forgetting the River Forth, the city of Stirling (and her beautiful castle), and the Ochil Hills.

"The top of the monument is actually called the Crown, created by Victorian craftsmen on the Abbey Craig in the 1860s. But one of our friends almost didn't make it to the top, the steps seeming to go on interminably, never-ending or, as William Wordsworth puts it, 'Continuous as the stars that shine and twinkle on the Milky Way.'

"With a bit of encouragement, however, she plodded on and was overjoyed to reach the Crown. Sometimes, we, too, have to plod on determinedly, despite life's hardships, to reach our final destination: Heaven. There, we will be crowned in glory and righteousness by the great King Himself, reigning in victory and in His presence forever and ever. There we will receive the crown of life that God has promised to those who love Him.

"The incredible news for us is that, spiritually speaking, everything is already sorted. Our futures are secure. God has anointed us, setting His seal of ownership on us, putting 'his Spirit in our hearts as a deposit, guaranteeing what is to come,' as it says in 2 Corinthians 1:21-22. For, make no mistake about it, Heaven is where total perfection and bliss abound."

Tim went on to share more about this theme of great joy, hope, and assurance for the Christian. When the sermon was over, Gabby was once more uncharacteristically quiet, obviously contemplating and thinking over all that had been said. Rose was again on her other side and immediately started to engage in conversation, taking Gabby's hand in hers.

Greg and I went over to a corner to pray. Eventually, Rose called us over. We were to get Pastor Tim immediately. In the next few minutes, our lives changed completely; for Gabby recommitted her life to the Lord, again asking Jesus into her heart, confessing her sins, praying for forgiveness, and promising to live anew. Tears flowed down her face—mine as well, for that matter. Praise the Lord! He really does answer prayer! This was, without a shadow of a doubt, the best, most brilliant part ever of all our time spent together. For spiritual birth had occurred, either in this moment or earlier at the summer camp many years ago. Gabby had been born again, elevated into the spiritual realm of God, receiving divine life and becoming a daughter of God.

It reminded me of the hot *mate* herbal drink I had once tried in Cusco, Peru. When the fresh herbs, or bags, had been added to the boiling water, there was a reaction, a change. The water was not the same as before, changing color, taste, and essence. It became good, delicious, and healthy! And in a sense, that was what had happened to Gabby. There was now a permanent infusion of God's Divine presence in her, bringing about change. She had become a new creation, receiving spiritual life and belongingness as one of God's spiritual children. And she would go on to develop a genuine love for God, for His people, and for everyone in the world. No wonder the gospel is referred to as good news of great joy in Luke 2:10. Today, even God's angels would be celebrating, as they do in Luke 15:7 and 10.

The tears flowed again back home. But once more, these were tears of joy and delight. We were all ecstatic, so happy for Gabby and for the decision she had just made. Things would not be totally smooth, by any means. But we would all be here for her, offering support, encouragement, love, and prayers as her new life developed. That night, we would call Hilda, telling her the good news. Then, I would be in Gabby's wondrous arms, receiving hugs and kisses. We would also pray together, giving thanks to God for His incredible grace and mercy.

The next day, we would visit the shop again to chat with staff, have a coffee and cake in the canteen, and have a last look at the latest fashions and trends, besides buying a few gifts for Hilda and for Stefan from one of the nearby men's outlets. We would drive out to Milford to see not only William McCrum's bust (and send a photo to Jinky and Didge) but also Hill Street and the house where Mom grew up. Indeed, we would spend quality time with the folks, chatting, laughing, chatting some more, drinking piping-hot tea, water, and Dad's Irish coffee . . .

And we had the best time of the year still to look forward to— Christmas, and Christmas in Germany, for that matter! The weeks and months would fly by. Life was good. Spiritual life was even better. No, there would be no sadness the next day. Only hope and joy and an exciting expectation for all that lay ahead, for all that the future would hold.

PART FOUR

CHAPTER 22
ROLL ON, THE HOLIDAYS!

Communication, and thus constant contact, is so important in a long-distance relationship. Thank goodness for social media! With not being able to be physically face-to face in person, we ensured we were in touch with each other on a regular basis in the weeks and months leading up to Christmas. Again, these were happy occasions, and thankfully, there were no difficult topics to broach this time around. Even the news about the Bauers was good. Gabby updated me on the phone.

"Mom's just returned from their house, Rob, and she's totally animated. You'll never guess what happened!"

"Go on, Gabs," I replied, "I can't wait to hear."

"Well, for one, the door was opened almost instantaneously. For another, she was greeted with a warm, generous, sincere smile and hug. For yet another, everything inside was neat and tidy; a small gas fire burned brightly; and there was even a delightful-looking Christmas tree standing proudly in one of the corners. But the change that brought the greatest joy to Mom's heart was the difference in Dieter's appearance: he had put on weight, and his eyes twinkled just as brightly as the lights on the tree!"

"Haha, Gabby, that's great to hear! I'm so happy for them. They've had to go through so much. It's impossible to imagine and appreciate the daily, constant pain and hurt they felt."

"That's not all, Rob! Menzel got the maximum sentence this time; he's going to prison for a long time."

"That's fair, Gabby, and just. So all the hard work paid off then, the petitions, interviews, and campaigning?"

"Yep, absolutely! Oh, I can't wait any longer to tell you. Mom said they started off sitting down by the fire sipping herbal tea and eating delicious gingerbread. You'll get a chance to try that out soon! However, all of a sudden, Hannah started crying. Mom, of course, immediately rushed over to give her a hug, expecting the worst. Anything but, Rob! Hannah said that they would never forget poor Max and Anna, but she's pregnant again! Due in July!"

"Yahoo," I shouted out joyfully into the phone. "That's wonderful news!"

"I know; I know. Mom can't believe it either. They are so changed from last time around, so much more optimistic, positive, and hopeful."

"That's great to hear. An optimistic state of mind is way better than a negative one, expecting positive outcomes instead of the opposite. We've both been there, battling through our Everest moments, through torment, brokenness, and affliction, struggling for survival, fighting for existence, plodding on day after day after day. Hope got us both through, along with friends and family. Let's not forget your Mom's part in all of this, Gabs; she helped to instill that hope into Hannah and Dieter, providing support, comfort, and a shoulder to cry on. Just like Dave and Jacqui did for me in my time of need."

"I know, Rob; I know. They've given her a nickname, by the way; she's their cherubic guardian angel! How nice is that? Mom said the three formed a tight-knit circle, everyone talking at once, bubbling over and over with *joie de vivre*! Rob, you remember how in Ireland I described you as a rock to stand on for support, encouragement, and reassurance? Well, I think I'd like to add to that. You're my cherubic angel!"

"Haha, Gabby, and you're the same for me. I think of you every single day. Hey, did you know angels need cuddles and kisses from time to time, just like anyone else?"

"Haha. You're not fooling me with that one! But don't worry; we'll soon be together again for Christmas, and you'll get your hugs and kisses then! Not long to go now, Rob."

"Can't wait, Gabs, can't wait. Roll on, the holidays! Roll on, Christmas!"

CHAPTER 23
CHRISTMAS

"Wow! What a change from the last time I was here, Gabby! Is it always this packed?"

"Sure is, Rob. These are the oldest and one of the biggest Christmas markets in Germany, dating back to 1393 and attracting over three million visitors each year. Look at the size of that Christmas tree!"

She was right—it was gigantic, standing almost one hundred feet high with quite literally thousands of lights, ribbons, and bells attached. We were back in the heart of Frankfurt's Old Town, in the iconic Römerberg Square, looking down at an incredible sight. For the place was alive, spilling over with a multitude of locals and tourists alike.

This was exactly how I imagined a Christmas market should be: there were stalls everywhere—over 240, in fact—selling their wares ranging from hand crafts and children's toys (such as rocking horses, dolls, and puzzles) to tree decorations of every imaginable type and design. Next came the huge variety of food options: everything from grilled bratwursts, roasted chestnuts and almonds, fries, potato fritters, and pancakes to crepes, waffles with cinnamon, chimney cakes, gingerbread, and confectionery—all washed down with *glühwein*, hot chocolate, chai latte, and so much more! This was a real smorgasbord of Christmas delights if ever there was one, and I loved it! The air was full of the fragrance and tang of Yuletide aromas.

Just then, Stefan and Ella appeared, panting heavily.

"Come quick, you two," gasped Stefan. "We managed to get tickets for the next carousel ride. Let's go!"

I just had time to admire the beautifully decorated wooden carvings on the merry-go-round before we were off, the music playing loudly and the horses bobbing up and down. On occasions like this, you really have to get into the spirit; so we did just that, whooping and shouting, leaning back as far as possible with legs sticking out at the front, laughing and giggling like the kids all around us.

Then it was time to try out that delicious deluxe hot chocolate, the perfect drink on a cold winter's day. An extra charge was made for the cute, bright, seasonally designed mug it was served in. But this was a one-off purchase and actually provided the perfect souvenir and memento for me to take home.

"Drink up, everyone," said Gabby. "I want to show Rob the incredible views from the cathedral tower."

We made our way slowly through the throngs of people, heading toward the Main River. There was still much to be seen en route: trumpeters on the rooftops competing with the church bells ringing out and the traditionally clad carol singers giving their all. The city really was in a completely festive mood. We finally made it to the cathedral, climbing the 368 steps to the top of the tower. But it was so worth the effort, for the views were indeed sensational. I finally got to appreciate the full size of these markets as Gabby pointed out the four linked areas, with the Römerplatz and Hauptwache forming the two main hubs. *What a beautiful city*, I thought to myself happily.

That night, and every subsequent one, I entered Gabby's room to pray. She had joined a small evangelical church and had matured greatly in her walk with the Lord, so much so that she was now praying out loud with confidence and faith and reading the Bible every day. We chatted for some time about answers to prayer and other themes from Scripture that interested us both. What a joy to be able to share in this way. This was going to be one of the best Christmases ever for me. And it only got better at breakfast the next day.

"We want to give you your Christmas presents early, Rob," said Gabby as we enjoyed freshly ground coffee with croissants and jam. "You'll see why in just a moment."

There were two to open—Gabby's first. It was another of those small, envelope-sized gifts, which were usually the best.

"Awesome! Perfect. Come here, you're getting a huge kiss for this!"

It was a ticket for that day's match against Bayern Munich. Next up, Stefan's—thicker, more like a parcel, which was quickly ripped open.

"Haha! That's brilliant, Stefan. I love it! Perfect, but no kiss for you!" It was a red, black, and white Eintrach Frankfurt scarf—ideal for that afternoon's game. "Thanks, guys. I really appreciate these, especially having taken the stadium tour. And against Bayern? Top match. Can't wait. Let's hope we win!"

It wasn't long before we were back on Tram 21, heading out to the stadium stop. This time, the carriage was totally packed, full of soccer fans en route to the stadium, including Gabby and myself, Stefan, and two of his friends. And lo and behold, who should we bump into but Karl and a friend of his!

"Hey, Karl, how's it going? You put on weight, man?" I asked.

"No, no," came his rather nervous reply.

In fact, I was pulling his leg, making him feel uncomfortable; for it was very obvious that his engorged stomach was not due to food or drink. He almost certainly had a red and white scarf stuffed inside, well out of sight!

"So, your team's ready for a whipping today?" asked Stefan, joining in the fun.

"No way. We'll beat you three to nothing, at least."

"Yeah, dream on, buddy," I said, proudly showing off my new scarf. But he hardly heard me, having scampered off like a dog with its tail between its legs. It was time for us to scamper off as well.

"These seats are brilliant, Gabs," I shouted into her ear. And shout it had to be, for the atmosphere was electric, and this before the match even began! We were seated quite close to the pitch and, while not exactly in the middle of the stand, close enough to give us good views of both ends.

"Look at the fans behind the goal, Rob," Gabby shouted back. They were all standing, linked together, jumping up and down and, along with the drum accompaniment, making quite a racket! But that was nothing compared to the crescendo that burst forth when the match kicked off—not just the noise from the fans but also the red, black, and white flares which were billowing out everywhere, forming a thick mist behind the goal. Soon, we, too, were on our feet, cheering loudly, for the Eagles had just scored a brilliant goal!

"Wow! German football is something else!" I shouted over to Stefan. He just gave me the thumbs up—he hadn't heard a word! In the end, Karl's prediction was totally wrong: Eintrach won two to one!

Hilda burst out laughing when we told her all about the day's events. I could see where Gabby got her spontaneity, natural impulse, and expression from. Like mother, like daughter, I had joked in Crete. And I wasn't wrong! They were like two peas in a pod—and I love peas!

Things only got better the next day when Gabby treated me to a surprise night out. We were back again in the heart of Frankfurt, in the Innenstadt District, standing outside the Opera House. The great, imposing building, surrounded by banks and cafés, looked stunning, as did the square in front, with benches to sit on to admire the pretty, lit-up fountains.

This popular classical music, entertainment, and conference center attracts almost half a million visitors annually and hosts some of the world's most famous conductors, soloists, ensembles, and orchestras, as well as the top jazz, chanson, and pop performers. Gabby had booked well in advance to get good seats and make sure it wasn't sold out.

"I wasn't quite sure if this was your cup of tea, Rob?" she asked, smiling sweetly and looking into my eyes as we enjoyed a pre-performance non-alcoholic cocktail down in the bar.

"I'm up for anything, love. It's a superb venue, and I've no doubt the performance will be just the same."

I wasn't wrong. The atmosphere in the Great Hall upstairs was rousing. The original Opera House was built in 1880; and although changes had to be made due to damage during the war, the inside still managed to retain many of the original features, including the beautiful mahogany paneling. And back in those days, they certainly knew a thing or two about sound—the acoustics were amazing!

We were here for the traditional Christmas concert, the symphony orchestra performing many well-known pieces from around the world. The hall was not overly large, resulting in superb views of, as well as a close proximity to, the performers, both of which just made the musical experience that much better. And best of all was the communal singing at the end. On came the lights; everyone stood up, interlocked arms, and began to sing their hearts out. No wonder the place erupted into rapturous applause after all that! The key to success, in my opinion, is all about audience participation—and they had nailed it!

Gabby was delighted at how well everything had turned out. It was all totally genuine on my part; for while classical music is not the norm for me, I do appreciate anything that is professionally presented, as was the case that night. Indeed, I'd once heard an outstanding recital by a blind Christian pianist which had left me totally spellbound.

"You're full of delightful surprises," I said, leaning over to kiss those fabulous lips. "I've really enjoyed myself. Thank you so much."

"I have, too. I love being with you—sharing, chatting . . . just doing things! Think this is going to be one of the best Christmases ever!"

We were both on the same wavelength about Christmas, and we were each proved right: incredibly delicious food; contented, cheerful, jovial moments with all the family; and, best of all, Christmas Day at Klaus and Lina's.

Traditionally in Germany, presents are opened on Christmas Eve. It was decided, however, to hold off until the twenty-fifth, when we would all be together, except for Ella. The elder Webers lived in a delightfully hilly suburb of Frankfurt: full of trees, bird life, open spaces and, best of all, stunning views from the living room and garden. In fact, that was our first stop as Klaus led us to the back of the house to admire the vista, made even better by the centerpiece of the grounds—a flowing fountain adorned in brightly shining Christmas lights. It was then a race inside to the heat to be greeted by Lina with not only the inevitable hugs and kisses but also with a drink. The house was overflowing with sweet-scented aromas of foods we were soon sampling: freshly made cinnamon, chocolate, and vanilla cookies, along with a delicious stollen cake full of marzipan, nuts, and raisins. With the additional smells from the homemade apple strudel and the slow-roasting goose in the oven, it was an aromatic heaven.

"Come through to the living room, everyone," said Klaus. "I think Santa has already been!"

We spent the next hour or so slowly opening presents one at a time. The gifts were not overly extravagant by any means; we had all agreed on a maximum price to spend per person so as not to overdo things. Indeed, some of the presents that brought the most joy and delight were the inexpensive ones. For example, Gabby had told me Klaus loved to play scrabble, so I had ordered a personalized scrabble mug with Klaus, Lina, and other family names etched into the letter spaces. He absolutely loved it. I, of course, had already received two gifts in advance.

But the highlight of the day was the meal, and I had been asked to prepare the starter. How on earth could I compete with Lina? Anyway, I would try my best, and it was only the appetizer, after all. First up was a juicy melon. I then used a Parisienne scoop to create perfectly rounded balls of fruit, which were placed on top of lettuce leaves. I add a few strips of crispy bacon, some Philadelphia cream cheese, a tomato and cucumber garnish, a few grapes, and presto!

Quick, easy, and delicious, if not exactly very Christmasy! I was off the hook! I could now relax and look forward to the main event.

"That was pretty good, Mr. Wilkinson," Gabby purred into my ear.

I very gently kissed her ear, then her cheek and lips. *Better stop there,* I thought. *Until later!* Everyone else seemed to enjoy the starter as well, asking me what the official name was. I'd found it online, but that was years ago. What in the world could I call it? Melon delight, fruit balls, cream cheese twist? I just went for "Parisienne cantaloupe with a twist." Everyone "oohed" and "aahed" as if it was the obvious answer. Actually, it was one of the first things that came into my head!

The star of the show was most definitely the stuffed roast goose, accompanied by red cabbage, a small bowl of Brussels sprouts (just for me!), and more of those incredibly delicious dumplings—a plump bread version, along with a potato variety. Fab-ul-ous! It got even better when the gravy was poured out on top.

"Oh, Lina, that's to die for!" I exclaimed. "I have never tasted gravy like this—so sweet and succulent! What have you got in there?"

"Well, it's a bit of a family secret, Rob. There are all the usual ingredients, of course—the giblets, neck, and fat of the goose, as well as stock, seasoning, shallots, a little butter, and finely grated potatoes to bind the sauce together. But for sweetness, I add some red currants, port wine, and freshly squeezed orange juice, giving it that zingy, fruity flavor. It actually goes well with all game meat, such as venison or even lamb."

"We usually have turkey for Christmas back home," I replied, "served with roast potatoes and bacon rolls filled with stuffing, sausages, and a port and cranberry sauce. The meat is delicious as well; Mom always buys the Norfolk Black variety, also known as

Black Spanish or Black Turkey, which contains less fat. She did say, though, that goose was extremely popular in Ireland in the days gone by. I can see now exactly why that was so!"

But more was still to come: Lina's own apple strudel, with ice cream or a white, custardy sauce or, in my case, both! What a meal! I was totally stuffed.

But now, just as at the Zudka restaurant, it was time for the toasts. First up was Klaus again.

"I'd like to make two toasts, if I may, both taken from the internet. The first one, Rob, is a rather somber one, a reflection on the wonderful memories of Christmases past. I will try not to get too emotional.

Just close your eyes and you will see

All the memories that you have of me

Just sit and relax and you will find

I'm really still there inside your mind

Don't cry for me now I am gone

For I am in the land of song

There is no pain, there is no fear

So dry away that silent tear

"S-sorry. It's very hard. I'll try and continue.

Don't think of me in the dark and cold

For here I am, no longer old

I'm in that place that's filled with love

Known to you all, as up above.[7]

Lina was on her feet now, bringing comfort and solace. In fact, we all were, gathered together in a huddle, condoling and consoling. I felt an inner glow in my heart, almost as if Julie was there with me, understanding, caring, loving. I was remembering her kind spirit, thoughtfulness, and tenderness. The tears flowed without stopping, and not just mine.

Eventually, Klaus was able to continue: "To a wonderful, amazing son, husband, dad, and friend. To Franz."

"To Franz," we all echoed.

"Okay, the second toast is a little easier to make. On a happier note,

'May you have the gladness of Christmas, which is hope

The spirit of Christmas, which is peace

The heart of Christmas, which is love.'[8]

Cheers, everyone!"

7   Gaynor Llewellyn, "A Silent Tear," Wattpad, Accessed September 30, 2024, http//www.wattpad.com/596989138-poems-a-silent-tear-gaynor-llewellyn.
8   Ada V. Hendricks, "May You Have," Pick Me Up Poetry, Accessed September 30, 2024, https//www.pickmeuppoetry.org/may-yu-have-by-ada-v-hendricks/.

We did just that, clapping and cheering heartily as well as raising our glasses to each other. Indeed, we had to have the hope, spirit, peace, and love that Christmas brings. It was so right to pause, reflect, cry, and reminisce. But both Franz and Julie would want us to be strong and happy and to keep on going. Yes, that glow in my heart was nudging me forward and onwards.

"Come on, Rob, you're always good for one. Up you get," shouted Stefan.

"Okay. Thank you. I'd actually like to make two toasts as well. The first one, of course, has to be from Ireland. I also found this one online.

The light of the Christmas star to you

The warmth of home and hearth to you

The cheer and good will of friends to you

The hope of a childlike heart to you

The joy of a thousand angels to you

The love of the Son and God's peace to you.[9]

The inevitable applause and cheering followed, so I had to wait before continuing. "The second toast is to our fabulous hosts today, Klaus and Lina, for their warm, generous hospitality and especially for that deliciously scrumptious, finger-licking, mouth-watering, so flavorsome, yummy, divine meal! Need I go on?"

---

9   Sherryl Woods, "Quotes by Sherryl Woods," Goodreads, Accessed September 30, 2024, https://www.goodreads.com/author/quotes/59446.Sherryl_Woods.

"Please do!" shouted a delighted Lina.

"To Lina and Klaus, everyone!"

"To Lina and Klaus!"

"And I have a small thank-you gift for you, Lina, all the way from Ireland." It came in a little square box wrapped in gift paper, which she eagerly ripped open. Inside was a piece of Irish crystal—a small Belleek vase. She was delighted and thanked me profusely.

"And I can't leave all the other ladies out," I continued. "So, here's one for Hilda and for my beloved, as well."

They both came in the same size box with identical gift wrap, Hilda's containing another little crystal vase. But when Gabby opened hers, it was different—a bit like a crystal tree trunk with branches shooting out in all directions. She took it out of the box and set it on the table.

"There's something wrapped up, hanging on one of the branches," she said, a little mystified. Then, she gently removed and opened it before giving out a massive shout. "It's a ring! Rob?"

I was already on my feet, having moved closer to her seat in anticipation, making the next part so much easier—getting down on one knee and taking her hand in mine.

"Gabby, I know we've only known each other for a short time. But to be honest, it feels like I've known you forever. You have changed my life, making me so happy, so content, so animated and high-spirited. I want this to go on forever, never-ending. I love your family. I adore *you*. Gabby Weber, will you marry me?"

She brought her hand to her mouth and let out an enormous cry. Then, it was another one of those "out of this world" moments when she lost it, diving onto me, knocking me flat on the floor. Meanwhile, everyone else had risen to their feet, now standing around us in a circle, chatting excitedly to one another; for, make no mistake, this had been a well-kept secret.

Eventually, when things began to calm down a little, Stefan spoke to Gabby: "You haven't answered Rob's question yet, sis!"

"Yes! It's yes—of course, I'll marry you, Rob. Oh, oh, oh! I love you deeply!" And she jumped on me again, kissing, hugging, laughing, crying—all par for the course for us both.

At long last, everyone was back seated around the table. I took the ring from the branchy tree stand, which was actually a ring holder, and put it on the appropriate finger. It fit perfectly. The ring contained a small green emerald, quainter and daintier than expensive, but most certainly a touch of Ireland.

"How did you know my finger size?" she almost whispered.

One finger pointed at Hilda said it all. She had been delighted when I told her my plans from Ireland on the last evening of Gabby's visit in October, and we'd been in close contact ever since. She had organized everything, right down to the bottle left outside in an outbuilding in an attempt to avoid any awkward questions if discovered in the fridge!

"Hope it hasn't frozen solid!" she joked as it was produced on a tray along with six thin flutes. When the glasses were filled, it was Hilda's turn to propose a toast—or two, rather, as she had to repeat it a second time in Spanish.

"To my new son, or should I say son-in-law? Welcome to the family, Rob. And to my beautiful, darling daughter, who means everything to me. I really love you both. To Gabby and Rob!"

"To Gabby and Rob!" everyone echoed back exuberantly and delightedly.

I gave my darling another kiss and asked her to join me in a rather important phone call to Armagh. But this was all about my new family, and I simply put the phone on speaker so everyone could hear and enjoy and take part in this happy, joyous moment.

Ah, it had gone so well. This time it had been easy for me to step off that "log" and propose to Gabby. Back in Crete, she had asked me my surname and if I liked kids. I had sensed undertones, that there was a deeper significance to the questions and, indeed, to my answers. I also remembered her reaction to Briege's reference to her as Mrs. Wilkinson.

"We must look the perfect couple, my love," I had said.

"We are the perfect couple!" she replied.

Yet again, en route to Ballintoy, I talked about the need to have someone special in my life to provide support and encouragement. She had then referred to me as that someone for her, that I was her rock and strength. But above all, as always with Gabby, it was in the eyes. They told me everything without the need for a single spoken word—that she loved me as much as I loved her; that we understood and were perfect for each other; that we wanted to spend the rest of our lives together; that right from that casual encounter in Crete, we were destined to be together; that both love and God had made it all happen, bringing us together as one.

Yes, this had definitely been the best Christmas ever.

CHAPTER 24
EASTER

It was the perfect day for a wedding. The sun shone brightly, with not a cloud in the sky. There was a slight breeze in the air, quite typical for this time of the year in Frankfurt. The photographer would be delighted, as would all the visitors from Ireland—Mom and Dad; Karen and Nathan; Greg and twelve other friends, relatives, and folks from church; two members of staff from the shop; and, of course, best man Dave with his gorgeous wife Jacqui. Add to that Tom and my sister-in-law Elena from Scotland, John Haley from Alfreton in Derbyshire, and the famous Boro lads (one of whom was en route to Stuttgart!); it was quite a cosmopolitan contingent!

The Danitz Arms Hotel was also the perfect choice for the wedding—chosen by Gabby and Hilda who, in fact, had organized nearly everything. I did the same for our honeymoon which, as requested, was to be yet another total surprise. The hotel was an old-world, traditional, mini-castle-type complex with a medium-sized ceremonial hall, exquisite décor, and, best of all, a fabulous old-fashioned staircase leading down to the banqueting area. The food wasn't bad either, by all accounts!

Very soon, the hall was filling up. All of Gabby's immediate family were present, of course, along with friends, relatives, and church and work colleagues. I stood proudly as the Lutheran minister smiled across at us; for Dave was once again by my side, ring in pocket, both of us men looking rather dapper, if the truth be told!

But this was nothing in comparison to the beauty who had just made an appearance at the back. I heard the "oohs" and "aahs" from everyone present but didn't dare turn around. Wagner's "Bridal Chorus" suddenly struck up on the organ as Gabby and Klaus made their way slowly down the aisle, eventually halting at the front, on the lefthand side. I could resist it no longer and looked over at the most glorious sight I had ever seen. She was ravishing and totally beguiling, radiating warmth, happiness, and love like an angel from Heaven. This was perfection and magnificence at its utmost, in its purest form. Then, she gave me that incredible smile of hers. Wow, this was paradise right here!

The ceremony progressed smoothly, and it was now time for the minister to pray for the exchange of rings: "Bless, O Lord, these rings as a symbol of the vows by which this woman and man have bound themselves to each other. Amen."

Dave passed me the ring, which I now placed on Gabby. "As this ring encircles your finger, so my love encircles you. As a ring has no end, so shall the love between us never cease. May it remind you always that you are surrounded by my love and that I will, at all times, be by your side. With it, I join my life to you, forever and ever. Amen."

Next, Gabby did the same, placing the ring on my finger and repeating the beautiful vows we had chosen together from some web pages.[10]

---

10   Based on vows from "12 Examples of Wedding Ring Exchange Wording for the Creative Officiant," American Marriage Ministries, http//www.theamm. org/articles/1703-12-examples-of-wedding-ring-exchange-wording-for-the-creative-officiant and "Ceremony Ideas," KimtheJP.com, http//www. kimthejp.com/ceremony-ideas (Ring).

Then, at last, the words I had been waiting to hear all day: "I now pronounce you husband and wife. You may now kiss each other."

It went a bit wild after that, as I kissed the most beautiful woman in the world with passion, fervor, and heartfelt excitement. After that, the spotlights were on, music blaring out, and confetti falling from above as we walked proudly back up the aisle, joined together in unity, oneness, and love!

Within no time at all, Mr. and Mrs. W were standing on top of that beautiful staircase, hand in hand, looking down at everyone who meant the world to us. I squeezed her hand. What a sight! What a setting and ambience—the stunning floral arrangements, the tables enchantingly decorated, the classical music from a string quartet adding and blending into the overall atmosphere and aura. We waited for the master of ceremonies to formally announce our arrival, the lights focusing in on the happy couple, the music blaring loudly as we descended slowly down the steps, stopping for photographs. It was then on to the head table to a fabulous meal, to funny and heartwarming speeches, to Klaus' inevitable toast, to the cutting of the cake, to the first dance . . .

What a perfect day! We were finally in the bridal suite, ecstatic and euphoric, already reminiscing over everything that had happened.

"You still haven't told me, my love, where we're going for our honeymoon," she said to me affectionately and tenderly.

"Well, I know we both like the warm weather . . ."

"Yes, indeed."

"It's between sixty-eight and eighty-six degrees Fahrenheit there just now! And we both like a top hotel with fabulous food . . ."

"Too right!"

"With maybe a few attractions to visit and tours thrown in, as well?"

"Perfect."

I handed her the envelope, which was immediately ripped open.

"The five-star Khalside Beach Resort Hotel. Aw, Rob, that's perfect! Dubai has been on my bucket list since . . . forever! Oh, you remembered that from Crete, didn't you? Oh, you're so adorable, Rob. I truly love you. Yahoo! I can't wait!"

"Good morning, beautiful," I whispered after gently brushing her lips with mine.

"Inside or out?" came her reply.

"Haha. You know the answer to that only too well. Thankfully, I now know every part of you and can say that you're gorgeous on both counts—inside and out!"

"Come here, Rob. Snuggle in a bit longer."

But it was true. Obviously, in love, the outside physical attraction plays a major part, the sensations and sensuality helping to bind and create feelings and emotions of happiness, contentedness, and satisfaction. You just can't get that person out of your head. It produces a need to spend time together: sharing, laughing, helping, supporting, encouraging, and sometimes consoling.

But the inner attraction is important as well—in the soul and in the heart: inner feelings of peace, oneness, genuineness, and sincerity—of caring for the person at a deeper level, of wanting the best for the person, and if need be, of wishing them to smile again, to be restored to their normal self.

Yes, love was the answer. We had both come to that conclusion on our last day together in the summer. Love would keep us together through thick and thin over the days, weeks, months, and years ahead.

However, it was not the full answer. There was something more to it which we had both recently begun to fully realize. It involved our spiritual natures; our deeper, inner souls; and our relationship with God. God was also the Answer. I had begun to learn that lesson a long time ago: that doing things on my own wasn't an option, that it simply didn't work. God had to be involved. I had to invite Him into my life at every twist and turn to provide encouragement, guidance, protection, blessing, and hope—no matter what I was going through. When Julie had passed, He helped me to keep on going. His presence sustained me. And ever since, I've tried to receive the blessing and power from those simple facts and promises.

He is here with me and with you. As we walk along our life-paths and journeys, holding His hand, we are in touch with Heaven. Unlike the illustration about the young children learning to water ski, He never, ever takes that hand away from us. He has His grip firmly on our shoulders. The powerful, mighty hand of God supports and strengthens us. He upholds us with His righteous right hand. Through the topsy-turvy of life, with all its ups and downs, bumps and knocks along the way, He never removes that stabilizing, supportive hand—the true hand of God. Herein lies our strength. Herein lies our security and confidence. He is with us. He is the Lord our God. He is on our side!

Yes, God brought us together. He knew I needed her, that I couldn't live on my own. "Two are better than one . . . A cord of three strands is not quickly broken," says Ecclesiastes 4:9. Gabby has become my partner in life, someone to share everything with, someone who loves me deeply, as she does the Lord. She wants to serve Him. What lies ahead is in God's hands. But we now face that together, stronger as a unit, a unit of three powerful strands.

Yes, love is an amazing thing, the most sensual experience in the world, bringing and creating fondness, patience, kindness, care and protection, trust and hope, respect, regard, attachment, endearment, unselfishness, faithfulness, intimacy, passion, and devotion. The two become one, entwined with each other. Just like us, as we come together: making memories, making dreams, making life, making a future together.

COMING SOON . . .
FATE

CHAPTER 1

Alaska is glorious in the summer. Between mid-June to mid-August, there are nearly twenty- four hours of sunshine, with temperatures varying between sixty to eighty degrees Fahrenheit, and very little rain. There are pristine National Parks to visit, extraordinary wildlife to view in their natural habitat, and a rich variety of activities to experience; such as hiking, kayaking, fishing and taking in the fabulous mountain and glacier wilderness landscapes on one of the world famous rail tours or boat excursions. Not to mention staying up late to watch the Midnight Sun, where the sun never seems to set![1]

Winter's another issue. Not for the travel agencies and adventurers, of course. There are the northern lights (aurora borealis) to imbibe, along with a smorgasbord of activities, ranging from skiing, snow mobile, sled and eco tours, hiking, photo treks, fat-tire biking, soaking in hot springs, and outdoor festivals, to mention just a few. Normally I would be up for any of these, but not today. The weather for me, in this instant was, put quite simply, totally and utterly unbearable, exceedingly annoying and immensely inconvenient. *I really shouldn't be here*, I thought to myself, as I looked up at the departure board in Fairbank's International Airport. One word stood out like a sore

---

1   https://www.alaskatours.com/summer-in-alaska

thumb: *cancelled, cancelled, cancelled.* Yep, my flight back to Anchorage gone, due to an incoming storm.

Why did I do it? Why did I come here at this time of the year? I asked myself again and again. Actually, it had been a very successful visit up until now. My best mate, Pete, wanted to build a log cabin, overlooking a beautiful lake, close to the Denali Natural Park Preserve, with its famous mountain (Denali, formerly Mount McKinley[2]), the tallest in North America, dominating the skyline. He was definitely on to something; in the summer the place would be teeming with wildlife such as birds, moose, and even the odd bear. Bird-lovers, hikers, photographers, de-stressors and many more, would flock here, if not for the incredible views, then simply to escape and to get away from it all.

I am a builder by trade, able to turn my hand to almost anything, and a pretty successful one at that, if I may say so. However, with winter setting in, work tended to tail off somewhat, and I'd found a window opening up for this visit. Hence the reccy; an opportunity to check out the location, about a two and a half hour drive south from Fairbanks, Alaska's second largest city. Local builders and suppliers, along with the logistics for the summer build, all had to be resourced.

I looked up at the board one last time, groaning outwardly. This was the worst case scenario. I had a four week contract starting on Monday, in one of the plush new hotels recently opened in Anchorage, catering for the thousands of visitors that were swarming to the region every summer. Future contracts would be inevitable, if all went according to plan. A late start, with the possibility of running over the completion date, was most definitely, not part of that plan.

---

2   From 1896 to 2015, it was known as Mount McKinley. The original name, used by the Native Athabaskan Indians, was restored in 2015.

I let out a loud sigh, looking round in desperation. Then I spotted it, a small sign in the corner: *Charters*. Worth a try, I thought, as I headed over. There were five small kiosks, four already with their shutters down. The one remaining had a rickety old sign that read: *Jake's Charters*.

The man behind the counter, who I assumed to be Jake, frowned when I asked the inevitable question.

"Yep, I'm going to Anchorage. But sorry man, the plane holds only four passengers. Seats all taken."

There was a softness in his face and a kindness in his voice that made me stay a while longer making small talk. Eventually he spotted my tool kit, asking the purpose of my visit. My lengthy reply, for some reason, brought an unexpected smile to his face. His next statements took me totally by surprise:

"Obviously, I'm Jake," he said, offering his hand.

"Dan, Dan Hewitt," I replied, extending my own hand for a firm, warm handshake.

"Dan, I've got a proposition for you. Well, more an offer; kind of like you scratch my back and I'll scratch yours. There's a small fold down seat in the luggage hold at the back of the plane which is rarely used, meant for a crew member, I reckon. Could offer you that, but no luggage. You'd have to leave your tools and belongings in the lockers behind me, probably till the next flight. Interested?"

"Too right, Jake! That's amazing! And in return?"

"Well, you mentioned about coming to work in the summer. I need some repairs done myself. Say a couple of full days of your time and we've got a deal?"

"Done! That's brilliant. I can't believe it!"

"It's small Dan, and in total darkness. You'd be in with all the backpacks and cargo; have three professional climbers on the return leg today. And we have to leave right now. There's an incoming storm; I'm literally taking off in the next five minutes. Go put your stuff in the locker and leg it as fast as you can!"

"Will do Jake," I replied en route. "And thanks ever so much, once again."

The four passengers were already aboard as I squeezed past apologetically, making my way to the cargo hold at the back. I quickly took in the cramped surroundings, with the aid of my mini flash light, which lived inside one of the buttoned pockets on my jacket. Backpacks and cargo crates had been tightly strapped in, and I was about to do the same when a sound from one of the crates distracted me. It was more like a low whimpering noise. On closer inspection, the culprit turned out to be a golden retriever puppy in a basket, along with doggie provisions in a separate compartment of the crate.

"Ah, you're so cute," I purred. "Wonder what your name is?"

I found it on the attached address label: *I'm Fate. Please deliver me to my new owner: Claire Gutiérrez, Portland Farm, Smitty's Cove, Whittier.*

The plane suddenly taxied out in preparation for takeoff, so I hastily found the small fold down seat in a corner and buckled up. Two minutes later, the small aircraft was air born. It should have been just over a one hour flight to Anchorage, a route, no doubt, that Jake had flown on countless occasions. Everything went according to plan for the first thirty minutes. It was quite turbulent, the wind outside loud and angry, growing in intensity as the minutes passed. But that was nothing to what happened next; the whole cabin suddenly came ablaze with a flashing light. This was followed by a thunderous, explosive noise, total blackness and then, worst of all, complete silence, apart from the howling wind outside. We had been struck by lightning and were literally falling from the sky. I remember Jake shouting out at the top of his voice that he was going to try to glide her down and attempt a crash landing. I remember feeling a total numbness as fear set in. I remember his final instructions to bend forward, embracing for impact. That was my final memory.

ABOUT THE AUTHOR

Robert Mark Walker worked as a missionary for Latin Link in Peru's Andes Mountains for over twelve years as a teacher, preacher, and lecturer. Born and bred in Northern Ireland, he now resides in Ayr, Scotland, attending Riverside Evangelical Church. He has a delightful Peruvian wife named Violeta and an amazing son, Greg, who has just completed his law degree.

Theological qualifications include a Masters in Theology from Aberdeen University, a Bachelors of Divinity from the University of London, and a Cambridge Diploma in Religious Studies from Cambridge University.

Ambassador International's mission is to magnify the Lord Jesus Christ and promote His Gospel through the written word.

We believe through the publication of Christian literature, Jesus Christ and His Word will be exalted, believers will be strengthened in their walk with Him, and the lost will be directed to Jesus Christ as the only way of salvation.

For more information about
AMBASSADOR INTERNATIONAL
please visit:

www.ambassador-international.com

Thank you for reading this book. Please consider leaving us a review on your social media, favorite retailer's website, Goodreads or Bookbub, or our website.

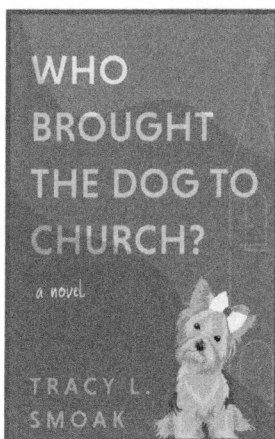

Printed in Great Britain
by Amazon

63089865R00117